Julie and the Too Hard Homework
Girls of the BryonySeries

Denise M. Baran-Unland

Cover Art by Jennifer Wainwright

This book is lovingly dedicated to the reader, whoever you might be.

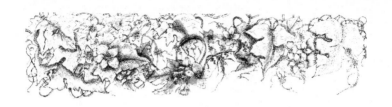

"I've got the key to my castle in the air, but whether I can unlock the door remains to be seen." – Jo March from "Little Women" by Louisa May Alcott

CONTENTS

CHAPTER 1: MORE THAN AN ORDINARY MOVIE

"Julie!" Mr. Drake called up the stairs. "Five minutes!"

'OK, Dad!" Julie called back.

Julie Drake chewed on the pink eraser of her yellow number two pencil and sighed. Three more boring long division problems to go. With a heavy heart, she closed her math book.

Ann always finished her homework on Friday night. But here was Julie, again, with her math book open on Saturday morning. Why did it take Julie forever to complete her schoolwork, especially math? She wasn't a baby anymore. She was in the sixth grade.

Julie stood and slowly stretched. Then she quickly smoothed the chenille bedspread over brass bed number one. Bed number two was for Ann or Katie when they spent the night. The beds had matching brown spreads and one tall dresser between them that had been Mr. Drake's when he was a boy. Her old scuffed wooden desk, full of schoolbooks, was on the opposite wall of the small room. Pleated curtains matched the beige rag rug on the board floors. The roof slanted. Three large hooks were screwed into the wall near the door for Julie's dresses and coats. Katie's room was bigger, but Katie had to share with her older sister Cara.

She glanced in the mirror above her dresser. Both braids still hung tightly in place. Julie loved short hair, but Mrs. Drake did not. The braids, at least, kept Julie's brown hair out of her brown eyes. Julie rubbed a peanut butter smudge off the corner of her cheek. She leaned down to pet the black kittens, Mittens and Muffy. They were curled up together on bed number two. A customer had given them to Mr. Drake. Mittens had white on her front paws. Muffy had a patch of white under her chin.

"Julie!" Mrs. Drake shouted. "Your father's waiting for you!"

"Coming!"

Julie picked up her lunch plate and sped down the stairs, through the living room, and into the kitchen.

Mrs. Drake was sliding a tray of chocolate chip cookies into the oven. The square kitchen scarcely had room for its round table, but it was the brightest room in the house. Late morning sunshine streamed through the east window and onto the polished wood floors and white walls, cupboards, counters, and the blue and white striped plates neatly stacked in the drying rack. Mrs. Drake was short and plump and wore her own long graying brown hair wrapped into an old-fashioned bun. She had a few wrinkles, and she usually smiled. But she wasn't smiling now.

Julie set her plate near the sink.

"Bye, Mom." Julie swiftly kissed Mrs. Drake's

cheek.

Mrs. Drake still didn't smile. "Well?"

Mr. Drake honked the horn.

"Bye, Mom!"

Julie sped out the back door and to the waiting car. The blue car wasn't a big car or a new car, but it was a car. Not everyone in Munsonville, a fishing village in northern Michigan, had a car, even though it was 1969 and most people owned cars. Julie's family was one of the lucky ones, even though the car wasn't new.

That's because Dad works for a used car lot, Julie thought smugly as she shut the door and reached for the seat belt. The Drakes also had a telephone, another rarity in Munsonville.

Munsonville also had a ghost – or so some villagers said. Julie didn't know what to think. Some days she believed in the ghost story; some days she didn't – and wished she could. She loved the idea of a ghost hanging around Munsonville.

"Hey, Jules," Mr. Drake said, and Julie glanced up at him.

Mr. Drake had wispy gray-brown hair that he combed over a tiny bald spot on the top of his head. He was shorter than Mrs. Drake but just as plump.

"Here." Mr. Drake handed Julie a five-dollar bill with a smile and wink. "Is this enough for 'extras?'"

"I think so."

Mr. Drake turned the ignition. "I have

branches, but no fruit, trunk, or leaves. What am I?"

"A bank," Julie said.

Mr. Drake sighed. "You've heard that one?"

"Last week, Dad."

As Mr. Drake backed out of the driveway, he frowned at the yard's blanket of autumn leaves.

"I should rake tomorrow afternoon," he said.

"I'll help," Julie promised.

"After your homework is done."

"I know," Julie said glumly.

Dad drove down Bass Street and then swung onto the next street and drove back up the hill. Munsonville's houses were built on a three-road hill. The smallest houses were near the bottom of the hill, the medium-sized houses were in the middle of the hill, and the largest and tallest of the houses stood at the top, near the cemetery and the woods.

Katie Miller lived inside a tall, three-story house on Blue Gill Road, the middle road. The boxy house had gray wood siding, green shutters, and chipped concrete steps. The back yard merged into the woods. Katie's family needed a big house. Katie had eight brothers and sisters, although not all of them lived at home anymore. Katie was the youngest.

"What movie are you seeing today, Jules?" Mr. Drake asked.

"'Pippi Longstocking,'" Julie quickly said. "I've read all the books."

Katie was sitting on the front steps, waiting

for them. She had a baby face, even at eleven, and short blonde hair, which she parted on the side and held in place with a pink plastic barrette. Her face brightened when she saw Mr. Drake's car. She jumped up, brushed leaf crumbs off her slacks, and ran to the driver's side.

"Hi Julie. Hi. Mr. Drake," Katie said breathlessly as she slid into the back seat.

Julie turned around. "Did you get your homework done?"

"Yep! Right after supper last night."

Julie turned away and looked out the window, her spirits sinking lower.

"So, Katie, you're seeing 'Pippi Longstocking?'" Mr. Drake asked as he started back down Blue Gill Road.

"Yes!"

"You sound very excited."

"I can't wait. I've read all the books."

Mr. Drake turned right and swung onto Pike Street. Ann Dalton lived halfway up in a small cream-colored square house with black shutters. Ann, too, was waiting for them on her front porch. Ann had thick black glasses and shoulder-length chestnut hair parted on the side. Julie didn't ask Brainy Ann if her homework was done. She knew the answer.

"I can't wait to see 'Pippi Longstocking,'" Ann said as she closed the car door. "I've read all the books."

Katie piped up. "Get your homework done?"

Ann gave a loud fake yawn. "Way before supper last night."

Julie folded her arms and narrowed her eyes. Mr. Drake drove down the hill and hummed to banjo music on the radio. Katie chatted to Ann about her new hairstyle magazine. The yards looked like one giant yard under their thick layers of crisp leaves. The maples and oaks burst with autumn radiance. She jealously watched a few leaves, light and oh-so-carefree, waft to the ground, and briefly wished she were an autumn leaf.

Mr. Drake turned right onto Main Street. To their left was Lake Munson, the fishing cabins, and Sue's Diner. To their right were a few brick buildings and a long wooden sidewalk. One building was Dalton's Dry Good's. Ann's parents owned it.

Julie scowled as they slowly rolled out of the village. Ann and Katie wouldn't think about school again until Sunday night. Only Julie...

It was a thirty-minute ride to Jenson. Mr. Drake turned up the radio. Katie and Ann's voices murmured under the music. Mr. Drake smiled and tapped his hand on the steering wheel as he drove. Julie watched the bare fields, feeling just as blah and empty.

Ordinarily, Julie loved the movies. Most folks in Munsonville, including Julie's family, didn't even own a television. They listened to programs on the radio.

But movies were different.

Movies showed the "bigness" of the world beyond Munsonville. Julie needed her imagination to listen to a radio program. But her imagination was limited. Julie couldn't imagine beyond pictures she'd seen in magazines or other movies because Julie had never visited most places.

Movies weren't like that.

Movies didn't depend on Julie's first-hand knowledge. Julie could just sit back, gaze up, and the adventure came to her. For two hours Julie could live in a world beyond her, a world that wasn't Munsonville.

For Julie was born in Munsonville. Her parents were born in Munsonville – and so were most of the people she knew and their parents, grandparents, too. Sometimes new people moved in. Hardly anyone moved out. That was Julie's unfortunate reality.

The movie theater was small with a large, flashing marquee. Big yellow lights announced, "Double Feature: 'Pippi Longstocking' and 'Under the Sea.'" The smaller lights glowed green: "Dream-Ghouls."

"Here we are!" Mr. Drake said cheerfully. "I'll pick you up at four. Have fun!"

"Thank you, Mr. Drake," Ann and Katie chimed as they slid out.

Julie gave her dad's cheek a peck and reached for the door handle.

"Hey, why the long face?" Mr. Drake said. "You like 'Pippi.'"

"You know why."

Mr. Drake gave her head an affectionate pat. "It'll work out, Jules. Don't dwell on it."

"OK."

Julie plodded to her friends, who'd already bought their tickets.

"Come on," Ann urged. "We're late."

"We still need popcorn and soda," Katie reminded her.

Julie took her place in the short line. She watched her friends smiling and chatting to each other. Her spirits sank lower.

"One ticket for the double feature," she finally said at the window.

"One dollar and fifty cents."

Julie handed the clerk the five-dollar bill. The clerk handed her a pink paper ticket and then counted out three one-dollar bills, a quarter, a dime, a nickel and five pennies into Julie's palm.

Julie trudged over the ugly tan and red carpet after her friends, who were already in the refreshment line but let her cut in. Popcorn was seventy-five cents. A soda was one dollar. That left one dollar and seventy-five cents for "extras."

"Ready?" Ann asked.

Katie nodded, giggling behind her hand. Ann said sternly, "Grow up, Katie."

One by one, they handed the usher their

tickets. He tore off the tops, handed them their stubs, and unhooked the cloth rope to let them pass.

Katie giggled again, loudly this time.

"Shut up," Ann hissed.

"Pippi Longstocking" was at the end. The girls ambled down the dim hall. Then Ann abruptly opened the door to "Dream-Ghouls", and everyone rushed inside, gasping under their breaths.

Haunting music played. Dark blue shadows rolled across the screen like ghosts over a lake. The credits started.

"Over here," Ann whispered, pointing to a side wall where nobody was sitting.

The girls quickly slipped into the row and scrunched into their red plush seats so no one would notice them.

"Oooh, I can't wait," Katie squealed under her breath.

"Shhh," Ann warned.

"Dream Ghouls" was about a man named Michael Morchester. Michael dreamed about ghouls every night – except now he was dreaming about ghouls in the daytime, too. No one under age seventeen was allowed to watch it.

But Brainy Ann thought kids' movies were childish. Katie loved a good scare even though she pretended she didn't. Julie was simply curious.

So while Ann stared at the screen and never moved, and while Katie trembled and whimpered, Julie became entranced with one of the characters:

Beverly Hartley, the man's psychologist.

Beverly Hartley was perfect.

She was blonde, poised, and very, very smart.

She wore her blonde hair brushed over the top of her head or pulled into a ponytail at the back of her head with a thick, wide barrette.

She wore tailored suits and pilgrim pumps, Michael's scary dreams did not frighten her. She knew all the right questions to ask. She had all the right answers.

And Michael always showed up at her door when he had nowhere else to turn.

Beverly Hartley was perfect.

When the movie ended, the girls headed to the restroom and then slipped into "Pippi Longstocking," for the final scene. They yawned and whispered to each other through "Under the Sea," a cartoon musical about a school for fish.

At four o'clock, Mr. Drake was waiting for them outside, just as he promised.

"How was 'Pippi Longstocking?'" he asked as they climbed into the car.

"Great!" Katie said just as Ann said, "Perfect," and Julie said, "Good."

"I know, I know." Mr. Drake grinned as he eased away from the curb. "Because you've read all the books."

Julie thought about Beverly Hartley all the way home. She was still thinking as she climbed the

stairs to her room. Muffy and Mittens blinked and stretched. Julie gave them a quick pat and then opened her bottom dresser drawer for the toy safe

Mr. and Mrs. Drake had given Julie the little safe last Christmas to encourage saving. Mrs. Drake believed Julie must earn every penny that went into the safe. So Julie earned money by helping Mrs. Drake with odd tasks, like rearranging the pantry and helping with canning. But Mr. Drake felt Julie deserved "extras."

Julie tucked the extra movie into the safe, spun the combination lock, and slid the safe back under sweaters. She sat on bed number two, absently petting Muffy, her mind in the movie.

At dinner, Julie picked at her fish loaf and mused on the Beverly Hartley parts of the movie.

Not until Mrs. Drake said, "Julie, are you ill?" did Julie realize she was at the kitchen table.

"Sorry, Mom." Julie set down her fork. "Just thinking."

Mr. Drake beamed. "Think about this, Jules. Where do you find a cow without legs?"

"I give up, Dad."

Mr. Drake pointed his fork at her. "Right where you left it!"

Mrs. Drake rolled her eyes and picked up her knife.

"May I please be excused?" Julie pushed her plate away.

Mrs. Drake nodded, buttering her roll.

But instead of sitting at her desk and working long division, Julie stood in front of her mirror, studying her reflection.

She covered her braids, cocked her head, and imagined she had blonde hair and an assured voice.

She imagined a golden nameplate on her door: *Julie Drake, psychologist.*

She held her head high and strolled up and down the short length of her bedroom in her best imitation of Beverly Hartley's confident stride.

She perched at the edge of her desk, picked up her notebook and number two pencil, and mouthed, "Please. Tell me about these dreams."

She pretended to hear and scribble little notes, nodding in wise understanding.

"Julie?" Mrs. Drake called out. "Ready for me to check your homework?"

She flew into her desk chair and opened her book. "Um, not yet!"

"Let me know."

"I will!"

Julie sharpened her pencil and scribbled out the next division problem.

CHAPTER 2: BAD NEWS FROM MRS. CLEMENTS

Julie finished her homework shortly after lunch on Sunday afternoon and joined Mr. Drake in the front yard. While they raked, piano music floated out the living room window.

Mrs. Drake was a good piano player. She played at church every Sunday. She gave piano lessons to Julie when Julie was a little girl. Julie loved piano music. But she hated piano lessons and "forgot" to practice. This led to many hot arguments between Julie and Mrs. Drake. Finally, Mrs. Drake gave up. Julie knew her mother secretly hoped Julie would change her mind. But that was as likely as frogs flying.

Still most people probably didn't rake leaves to the lively sound Mozart's "Rondo Alla Turca."

"Ready, Jules?" Mr. Drake called from across the yard through his cupped hands.

She stopped raking. Mr. Drake had pushed his leaves into a huge pile and was standing beside it, beaming. His cheeks were shiny and red with the chilly air and excitement.

"Sure, Dad."

Julie dropped her rake, jogged to the pile, and half-heartedly skidded into its side, scattering leaves everywhere. Mr. Drake sighed and shook his head as Julie stood and brushed leaf crumbs off her blue corduroy slacks.

"Well, you're out of practice. Hey, what did one leaf say to the other?"

"Please leaf me alone."

Mr. Drake's face fell.

"You told me that one last week, Dad."

He brightened. "How about this one? What did the boy leaf say to the girl leaf?"

Julie shrugged.

"I'm falling for you." Mr. Drake tickled her ribs. "Get it?"

"Very funny, Dad."

Julie walked back to her rake, picked it up, and surveyed the rest of the yard. Plenty more leaves to rake, plenty more time to be Beverly Hartley.

"What do you think, Mother?" Mr. Drake said half an hour later when Mrs. Drake opened the door to check their progress. "Should we roast hot dogs tonight?"

"That would be fine."

What do psychologists in big cities eat, Julie wondered. Probably not hot dogs. Steak, maybe?

"And marshmallows? Mother?"

Mr. Drake burned the leaves in front of the house while Mrs. Drake lit a campfire in the backyard pit. As the sun set and the air cooled, they sat on old logs and slowly charred their hot dogs while the fire warmed their faces. They ate the crisp dogs in cool soft buns at the old wooden picnic table. They ate cold potato salad and cole slaw Mrs. Drake

had prepared that morning.

Mr. Drake talked about the car lot. Mrs. Drake murmured here and there and nodded her head. Julie half-listened, her mind on Beverly Hartley. She'd ask Katie's brothers what people ate in the city. They'd gone to college. They'd know.

Katie showed up just as Mrs. Drake opened the bag of marshmallows.

"Yummy!" Katie cried.

"Have one." Mr. Drake handed her a sharpened stick. "Or two."

Katie happily speared a marshmallow and settled on a log next to Julie.

"Hey, Katie," Mr. Drake said. "Did you hear about the hot dog that asked the ketchup for a date?"

"Nope!"

Mr. Drake snickered. "He mustard up the courage."

Katie laughed. Julie groaned. Mrs. Drake sighed loudly and reached for the marshmallow bag.

"What's the opposite of a hot dog?"

Katie thought a moment. "I give up."

"A pupsicle!"

"Mom," Julie interrupted. "May I go to the library after school tomorrow?"

"You may. But don't dawdle. You need time to complete your homework."

"I know, Mom."

"I'll go with you," Katie mumbled around her

mouth full of marshmallow.

Julie shook her head. "Not this time. I'm researching a project."

Katie gasped and grabbed Julie's arm. "The...the ghost?"

"No, not the ghost."

Katie's shoulders sagged. "Well, if you do research the ghost, I want to help."

"OK."

Munsonville Library wasn't very large, about the size of Joe's General Store. Nevertheless, Munsonville Library held plenty of books and useful information – maybe even information useful to Julie. She paused at the circulation desk, holding her vinyl tote bag by its plastic handle. She studied the dark paneled walls, ten rows of green-painted bookshelves, round tables with wooden chairs, and one overstuffed couch. Where should she start?

"Julie?"

A brown-haired woman in a gray-tweed skirt, beige blouse, and glasses hanging on a chain around her neck stepped away from the counter, carrying an armful of books.

"Julie, are you looking for something in particular?"

"Um...yes."

"And what is that?"

Julie blushed and hung her head, suddenly embarrassed about her Beverly Hartley daydreams. Maybe, she thought, maybe I should just go home.

"Julie?"

She raised her head and looked at Mrs. Clements' kind eyes. She took a deep breath. You can do it, Julie told herself. Go on. Ask.

"Do you, um, have any books on psychology?"

Mrs. Clements raised an eyebrow.

Julie's face grew hot.

Mrs. Clements jerked her head at the tables.

"Julie, have a seat. I'll put the books away and come right back."

"OK."

Julie felt like running away. But that wouldn't help now. She'd already opened her big mouth.

She plodded to the table, dropped into a chair, and set her tote bag next to her. She couldn't stay long. She had tons of homework. Brainy Ann was surely long done. Katie probably was, too.

Mrs. Clements drew up a chair.

"I'm sorry to keep you waiting, dear," Mrs. Clements said. "Now what kind of psychology books do you need? Is this for a class project?"

Julie started to say, "Yes," and then stopped herself. No point in lying. Everyone talked to everyone in Munsonville about everything. Her mother would eventually find out.

So Julie shook her head. "No, I want information for myself."

Mrs. Clements cocked her head, puzzled.

Julie took another deep breath. "I want to be a psychologist."

There. She did it. Now someone knew what an idiot she was.

Julie's heart pounded hard.

Mrs. Clements smiled, a warm, encouraging smile. Julie relaxed, a little.

"That's a very ambitious goal, Julie."

"I want to help people," Julie blurted out and then realized it was true.

Sure, Julie wanted to be beautiful and poised like Beverly Hartley instead living the rest of her life like fishing village Julie with two braids. But Julie, who really had a big heart, also wanted to be smart enough to help people solve their problems.

She wanted to be smart problem-solver like Beverly Hartley.

"Well, four years of college is a must. How are your grades?"

Julie hesitated. "Pretty good."

That wasn't a lie. Julie's grades were average, above average sometimes. But Julie worked very, very hard to earn those grades.

Julie mentally added it up.

She was nearly three years away from high school. High school was four years. Then she'd need four more years of college.

The thought of years and years and years of homework made her head hurt.

"I'm glad to hear it," Mrs. Clements said.

"College is very expensive. Still, students with good grades can earn scholarships."

"What's a scholarship?"

"A scholarship pays for part – or all – of college tuition. But scholarships are very competitive. Only top students receive them."

Julie's head whirled at the crushing news. Her throat felt tight too tight to breathe. Top students? Julie would never be a top student!

"Thanks, Mrs. Clements," Julie choked out, grabbing her tote bag. "I have to go. Lots of homework."

Mrs. Clements rose, too. "I'm always happy to help, Julie."

Julie fought back tears as she trudged up Bass Street toward home. All weekend she had lived inside her bubble of make-believe joy.

And now – BOOM!

She hadn't floated down to reality. She'd landed with a hard exploding thump. What a goon she was!

No one in Munsonville went to college. OK, Katie's brothers Al and Ben went. But they had boring teacher jobs in Jenson, not an exciting place like Detroit or Chicago. They still came home for Sunday dinner. Why did Julie ever think she could be different? Because of a stupid movie she wasn't allowed to see?

Mrs. Drake was painting the top of her meatloaf with ketchup when Julie stumbled through

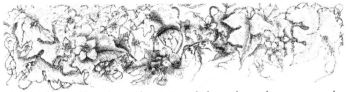

the door. She hastily wiped her hands across her apron and reached for a glass and small plate.

"I made cookies," Mrs. Drake said as she set a glass and a plate on the table.

"Thanks, Mom," Julie mumbled as she hurried past. "I'm not hungry."

"Julie, are you ill?" Mrs. Drake called after her. "Does your stomach hurt?"

"No, Mom."

"But you love cookies and milk!"

Julie rushed up the stairs and burst into her tears before she'd completely shut the door. She threw herself on bed number one, crying into her pillow so no one could hear.

She pictured Ann reading a book and Katie coloring while her older sister Cara practiced her singing. Julie hadn't even started her homework because Julie had gone to the library, thinking she could be a psychologist. Now she had a mountain of homework and a smashed dream.

Julie cried and cried and cried, kicking her legs and clutching the pillow. She cried because she had so much homework to do; she cried because she wasn't beautiful and smart; she cried because she lived in a backwoods fishing village instead of a bustling city; she cried because she had no hope.

Finally, Julie lay still, her pounding head still buried. Julie was out of tears. But the image she'd created for herself, *Julie Drake, psychologist,* still burned in her mind, even as her eyes and throat

burned, and her nose dripped, and her face felt wet and puffy.

Julie rolled onto her side and curled up like a baby, but she couldn't stop the thoughts; a new Julie was taking shape. This Julie was an accomplished, self-assured psychologist, a Julie who shared her hard-earned wisdom to the people she helped. This wasn't a blonde Beverly Hartley-type of Julie in tailed suits and pilgrim pumps to match. This Julie was a brunette with a page boy haircut, and she wore a tailored pants suits and high heels, clothes no one wore in Munsonville, clothes people wore in movies and magazines.

The image was clear to Julie, yet too far away to grasp. But with Julie's initial disappointment washed away, Julie saw what she did not see earlier.

To help others, Julie must first help herself.

"Jules," Mr. Drake called up the stairs. "Dinnertime!"

Julie sniffed, pulled herself up, and wiped her dripping nose on the back of her hand.

"Coming!" Julie called back.

Well, she couldn't go to the dinner table looking like a mess. Julie pulled the rubber bands from her braids and ran her fingers through the tangles. The act untangled something inside of Julie, too. She felt calm, resolved.

Julie leaped off the bed, dashed to the mirror for a comb, and rebraided her hair with practiced,

nimble fingers. When she tied the last blue ribbon, she set the comb in its place, straightened her shoulders, and turned around, her gaze landing on the stack of books on her desk.

"We can do this," Julie told them. "We can do this together."

Julie marched into the bathroom to wash her hands and face. Then she headed downstairs to eat her first dinner as the new Julie.

CHAPTER 3: A BETTER MIND

"Sam, I'm worried about her."

"Mother, it's Jules. She'll be fine."

Julie was just leaving the bathroom when she heard her parents' voices."

"Maybe she needs a checkup. Or a tonic. You know what? I'll make an appointment with Dr. Rothgard right now."

"Mother, I think..."

Their voices trailed away. Julie tiptoed to her room and softly shut the door. She knew why they were talking about her. They didn't like all the hours she spent studying.

But they didn't understand.

And Julie didn't care.

She needed college to become a psychologist.

She needed good grades to get into college.

And Julie wouldn't improve those grades without lots and lots of studying.

She didn't have time to work puzzles with her parents on school nights in the small, cozy living room with its overstuffed couch and overstuffed chairs, huddled around the coffee table and sorting through pieces. She didn't have time to play cribbage with them on Friday nights at the small kitchen table in the brightly lit kitchen while mouthwatering smells of their good dinner lingered in the air. She bet Beverly Hartley never played cribbage or put together a thousand-piece puzzle of

the mountains with *her* parents.

"So which one did you like best?" Mrs. Clements asked Monday afternoon as Julie set her stack of library books on the counter.

"I didn't read them."

"Why, Julie! I thought you liked ghost stories."

"I do. But I'm busy studying. I don't have time for ghost stories."

"Why all the extra Homework?"

Julie sighed Inside, impatient to be on her way. "It's not extra homework. I want to improve my grades."

A woman with two little girls set six board books on the counter. Mrs. Clements picked up a pen and began removing the due date cards from their jackets.

"Well, try not to study so hard, dear."

"Thanks, Mrs. Clements."

Julie checked the wall clock as she zipped up her jacket. She lost five whole minutes. She'd better run home.

"I made cookies," Mrs. Drake said as Julie burst through the door.

"Thanks, Mom," Julie said breathlessly as she sped toward the stairs. "I'm not hungry."

"But Julie..." Mrs. Drake's voice called after her. But Julie didn't stop until she'd reached her room and shut her door.

Soon, Julie was sitting at her desk,

surrounded by books, and diagramming sentences into her spiral-bound notebook.

At the dinner table, Julie mentally drew a map of the area near the Panama Canal, since that was due tomorrow, too. If she sketched it in her head now, she could quickly...

"What?" Julie asked.

"I said, 'Would you like more meatloaf?'" Mrs. Drake repeated in a crisp voice.

"No, thanks, Mom." Julie set her napkin beside her plate. "Please, may I be excused?"

"Wait," Mr. Drake said.

Julie waited, squirming with impatience.

Mr. Drake grinned. "What do Alexander the Great and Winnie the Pooh have in common?"

"I give up, Dad."

"Same middle name!" Mr. Drake laughed out loud. "Get it?"

"Got it. May I be excused now?"

Grinning, Mr. Drake pointed to the door. "Go! Get out of here!"

"Thanks, Dad."

As Julie dashed to the stairs, she heard vague whispers and one clear sentence: "Mother, it will blow over."

Julie worked complex fractions that night until her eyes prickled, and her brain softened...

With a start, Julie dropped her pencil.
Huh?

Dropped her pencil?

Had she fallen asleep? For how long, Julie thought with a surge of panic.

She crawled under the desk to grab the runway pencil and crawled back out, flustered, disheveled, her eyes searching out the alarm clock on her dresser.

Ten o'clock??? How – when...???

She flew to her clock; with trembling fingers, she set the timer back an hour. Then she passed out on bed number two with the cats, fully dressed.

"You're awfully quiet today," Ann said at lunch the next day as she poked Julie in the ribs.

Julie picked up her meatloaf sandwich.

"Just a little tired," Julie said, stifling a yawn and taking a bite.

Katie giggled as she glanced at Ann. "Bet she falls asleep first."

"Probably."

"Huh?" Julie asked.

"Friday night, silly," Katie said. "Aren't you sleeping over?"

Julie moaned inside. She had forgotten about Katie's slumber party.

"I can't," Julie said. "I have to study."

"Study before dinner," Ann suggested.

"I said, 'I can't.'"

Ann shrugged. "Your loss."

"Noooo!" Katie wailed. "Julie, you promised!"

Julie picked up her tray and glared at Ann. "Sorry I'm not as brainy as you."

"What?" Ann narrowed her eyes. "Are you picking a fight? Take it back!"

Julie stalked away as Katie cried, "Julie, come back!"

But Julie kept walking, feeling more and more stupid with each step. She dumped her scraps into the garbage can and almost slammed the tray on the counter.

She was less angry at Ann than she was at herself.

C+

That was the grade in big red ink at the top of her math test.

All those hours and hours of studying.

All those hateful, extra practice problems.

And all Julie did was move her grade from a "C" to a "C+."

She hated her life.

In English class later that afternoon, Katie slipped Julie a note: *Please don't be mad. It's OK if you have to study.*

Julie scowled as she slid Katie's note into her history textbook. That was easy for Katie to say.

Katie wasn't brainy like Ann, but Katie didn't struggle with school, either. If Katie got stuck, her two older teacher brothers helped her. If Julie got

stuck, Julie had only herself.

"I made cookies," Mrs. Drake said as removed a carton of milk from the refrigerator.

"Thanks, Mom," Julie said as she plodded through the room to the stairs. "I'm not hungry."

Maybe I should wake up an hour early every day to study, she thought as she climbed. Maybe if she spent an extra hour every day to study, Julie could push that C+ to a B.

"What time is Katie's party?" Mr. Drake asked Thursday as he passed the fish cakes to Mrs. Drake. "Do you need a ride after dinner or are you eating your fill of pizza pies?"

"I'm not going," Julie said, trying not to yawn as she cut her cake in half with her fork.

"Not going?" Mrs. Drake echoed. "Why, Julie, it's Katie's birthday. She's expecting you."

"I have to get my grades up, Mom."

Mr. Drake cleared his throat. "Jules..."

"I don't need a lecture, Dad."

Mr. Drake glanced at Mrs. Drake and then back at Julie. "Are you in trouble at school?"

"No, Dad." Julie sighed in exasperation.

"Then why the extra studying?"

Julie looked down at her plate.

"Julie?"

"I have a goal," Julie mumbled.

"You do?" Mr. Drake asked, perplexed.

"A goal?" Mrs. Drake echoed, looking concerned. "What kind of goal?"

"College.".

Mr. Drake burst out laughing. Julie threw down her napkin.

"I hate you!" she gasped out as she ran from the room.

"Julie!" her mother called.

But Julie ignored her. She flew up the stairs, slammed her door, startling the sleeping cats, and locked it. She threw herself onto bed number one, sobbing and kicking her legs.

All those weeks of hard work.

For a C+!

She was stupid.

She was a nobody.

Her own father had laughed at her!

Well, the whole world should laugh at her. *Julie Drake, psychologist.* Ha!

Julie cried harder.

After a long while, Julie heard a soft knock on the door. She ignored it.

"Jules," Mr. Drake said in low voice.

"Go away!"

"Jules, open the door."

Mr. Drake had used "that tone." He meant business, and Julie knew it. Julie had to get up with her puffy, tear-streaked, stupid face and open the door because she was eleven, and he was the grownup.

Julie slid off the bed and opened the door.

"May I come in?" he asked sheepishly.

Julie shrugged and flopped onto the bed. Mr. Drake's eyes roamed over Julie's desk: scattered books, open notebooks, wadded papers, pencils, and pencil shavings.

Then he sat at the edge of her desk chair. His cheeks were pink from embarrassment. He looked as if he might cry.

"Say it, Dad."

"I...I shouldn't have laughed."

Julie crossed her arms and looked away.

"I shouldn't have laughed," Dad repeated. "But...but...who's filling your head with college? Are Katie's brothers getting uppity? Maybe I should go over there and tell them to mind their own..."

"Me!"

Mr. Drake blinked. "You – what?"

"Me. I put the idea of college in my head."

Mr. Drake looked dazed. He blinked three times. He rubbed his forehead.

"You?" Mr. Drake repeated.

"Yeah, Dad. I know what you're thinking, 'How did a girl as stupid as me come up with college?'"

"Watch your mouth, Julie Girl!"

Now it was Julie's turn to blink. Her father was the most easy-going, mild-mannered person she knew. He rarely raised his voice. If any yelling was needed, Mrs. Drake did it for him.

"Then why act all surprised?"

"Because...well, because we're not a college

family, Jules."

"So I can't be the first?"

"I didn't say that."

"Then what are you saying, Dad?"

Mr. Drake sighed and ran a hand over his balding head. "What I'm saying Jules, is that college is a big decision."

"Too big for me?"

"Watch your tone, young lady. I'm losing my patience with you."

Mr. Drake never lost his patience either. Julie knew she was really in trouble.

He rubbed his double chin for a few minutes.

"It's not just grades, Jules. It's planning for tuition costs. It's choosing the right classes. Have you considered any of this?"

"That's why I'm studying so much, Dad."

"It also takes a certain...type...of person to attend college, Jules. Not everyone is that type."

"Only smart, rich people can go to college?"

Mr. Drake sighed. This time he rubbed his whole face before speaking. "Let me ask you this, Jules. Why do you want to attend college?"

To become a psychologist, Julie said to herself. But she wouldn't say it out loud. She'd sound like an idiot. So she said, "For a better mind."

"A better..." Mr. Drake's face contorted, and he bit his lip to keep from laughing, but his shoulders shook anyway. "Listen, Jules. Have I ever complained about your grades?"

"Mom always says, 'I don't work to my full potential,'" Julie said in her mother's tone.

She and Mr. Drake both chuckled, which eased the tension in the room.

"There's more to my Julie Girl than her grades," Mr. Drake said. "And there's more than one way to better your mind. Look at all the library books you read!"

Used to read, Julie silently corrected him.

"You're a smart girl, Jules. But not all smartness comes from books. As long as you're completing your assignments, I'm pleased. And at the end of the day, your mother is, too."

"But that won't get me into college!"

"You don't need college to get married and raise a family." Mr. Drake reached out and ruffled the top of Julie's head. "At least, not the last time I looked. Now, what's the opposite of irony?"

Julie looked down, her heart sinking.

"Wrinkly," he guffawed. "Get it?"

Julie wrenched away.

"That's the problem, Dad! Maybe I don't want to 'just' get married and raise a family! Maybe I want a career!"

Mr. Drake's jaw dropped.

He looked at Julie as if she'd grown tentacles out of her head.

But he only stammered, "Sure, Jules. I mean, your mother has a career."

"Dad, working the front desk at Munsonville

Inn two days a week when I'm in school isn't a career!"

Mr. Drake's face sagged. He rose unsteadily to his feet. "Think on it some more, wouldja, Jules?"

"I..."

But Mr. Drake had already left the room, closing the door behind him.

Julie scampered to the door and cracked it open. She heard her father say, "Mother, where do girls these days get such outlandish ideas?"

Julie shut the door, and fresh determination rose inside her.

"Here," Julie patted her heart. "Right here."

No longer tired or discouraged, Julie settled down at her desk and attacked her homework with renewed vigor.

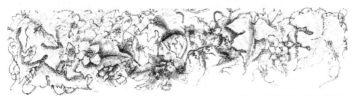

CHAPTER 4: SHE HAS A NAME, YOU KNOW

"I'm glad you changed your mind," Katie said as she untied Julie's braids. All three girls sat cross-legged on Katie's twin bed. "We have more fun with you."

I didn't change my mind, Julie thought. My parents made me.

Ann cocked her head. "Is it Julie who's fun — or her hair?"

"Both," Katie giggled.

Katie's bedroom was so different from Julie's. Both the slanted roof and the floors were painted white. Photos from hairstyling magazines covered most of the plaster walls on Katie's side of the room. Katie's room had two beds, too. But one of those beds was Cara's. Sheets hung across a steel pole running across the ceiling, to give each girl privacy. That didn't matter tonight. Cara was sleeping on the couch so the girls could use the whole room — and her bed.

Julie pointed to Katie's hairstyle magazine, which lay open and upside down on the bed. "Which one this time?"

Katie flipped it over and pointed to a woman with high, back-combed hair. "This. I'm practicing teasing. Hand me the comb."

Julie did, and soon Katie was tugging away.

"Anyone see the ghost today?" Katie asked.

Ann's blue eyes were stern. "There's no ghost. Grow up, Katie."

"Who says?" Julie countered, rushing to Katie's defense. "Plenty of people have..."

"...have said they've seen shadows at Simons Mansion," Ann said, shaking her head as if Julie were a small child.

"And heard piano music," Katie chimed in.

"People see and hear what they want to see hear and hear," Ann said. "And believe what they want to believe."

"Ow!" Julie's hand flew up to her head. She turned around and glared at Katie. "Be careful!"

"I'm trying! But your hair's so tangled."

"Can't help it," Julie said. "Long hair wasn't my idea. I really want..."

"A page boy," Ann interrupted. "We know."

"But it's sooo romantic," Katie breathed.

"A page boy?" Ann made a face.

"No, silly. John Simons. A world-famous piano player marrying a Munsonville girl and building her a mansion up on a hill in the woods."

"She died two years later," Julie said scornfully. "Giving birth. That doesn't sound very romantic to me."

"But he wrote a song for her!" Katie cried. "And he played it at end of every concert! He planted pink bryony all over the estate for her. Back in Victorian times. With ball dresses and top hats. That's very romantic!"

"Big deal," Julie said. "He skipped town as soon as she died and never came back."

"But he did come back!" Katie insisted. "He came back after he died."

"There's no ghost, Katie," Ann repeated.

Julie turned on Ann. "How do you know? How do you know for sure John Simons isn't haunting his mansion?"

Ann shrugged. "And all that 'romantic' pink bryony is poisonous. Steve hates cutting the grass up on that hill."

Steve Barnes was the village maintenance man. He kept the entire village looking its best, including the area around the abandoned mansion.

"Steve's too nice to hate anything!" Katie cried. "I don't believe you, Ann Dalton!"

"I heard Dad tell Mom," Ann tossed her head. "And I'm smarter than Bryony ever was. When I marry someone rich and famous, I'll move far, far away. I'll own homes in three countries and eat steak every night. You won't find me sticking around this stupid village."

Not me, Julie thought glumly. I'll be baking cookies and working the desk at Munsonville Inn.

Katie shook the can of hairspray and sprayed a thick cloud over Julie's head, making everyone cough and cough and cough and cough and cough.

"Open a window!" Ann choked out.

Katie ran to the window.

Julie buried her face in Katie's blanket.

Soon a light breeze filled the room. The girls' barking soon returned to normal breathing that only stung a little.

"How much did you use?" Ann demanded.

Katie sheepishly held up the pink can. "Not much. Just half."

Julie slept restlessly in Cara's bed that night, dreaming she was feeding cookies and milk to a dozen children with coughs and runny noses while trying to register a guest at the Munsonville Inn.

She woke up, heart racing and full of determination to change her fate.

After a quick breakfast of toaster waffles, chocolate milk, and an apple, Julie left her friends in front of Saturday cartoons and headed down to the library. She smiled as her shoes scuffled through the crispy leaves and held her head high. These were the first footsteps of her new knowledge.

The library was just opening when Julie and her tote bag with last night's clothes arrived. Mrs. Clements was still taking off her coat.

"Julie, what a surprise! You're up early."

"Can you help me find a book?"

"Of course." Mrs. Clements grabbed a ballpoint pen and a scrap of paper. "What's the title? If we don't have it, I can request it from the library in Jenson or Evansville."

"I don't have a title to give you."

Mrs. Clements, pencil poised over the paper. "Well, then, tell me a little about the book. I might

know it."

Julie blushed very deeply. "Mrs. Clements, I need to start learning about psychology. But I don't know where to start."

She braced herself for Mrs. Clements' laugh. Instead, Mrs. Clements face softened. She set down her pen. "Come with me, Julie."

Julie followed Mrs. Clements to the reference section. Mrs. Clements selected a dictionary and handed it to Julie.

"Look up 'psychology' and tell me what it says," Mrs. Clements said.

What did Mrs. Clements think Julie was — a baby? Still, Julie flipped to the correct word. If she didn't, maybe Mrs. Clements wouldn't help her.

"'Psychology: the science or study of the mind and behavior,'" Julie read loud.

"Exactly. To be a psychologist means to be a person who understands human minds and human behavior."

"How do I learn? Before college, I mean."

Mrs. Clements smiled. "Come with me."

Julie followed Mrs. Clements to the periodical section. Mrs. Clements opened a drawer marked "April 1968," pulled out a newspaper, and headed to the front desk. Again, Julie followed.

"Wait!" Julie objected when Mrs. Clements raised the lid of the copy machine. "I didn't bring ten cents."

Mrs. Clements smiled again and handed Julie

the copy. "This one's on me."

Julie looked at the headline: "How Discrimination Feels." What did *that* have to do with psychology? Mrs. Clements was no help at all.

But Julie couldn't say that. After all, Mrs. Clements had just paid to copy it.

So Julie looked up at her and said weakly, "Thank you, Mrs. Clements."

Julie slid the clipping into her tote bag and trudged out of the library and over to Bass Street, dragging feet of lead. Each crunch of each leaf mocked her: *First step of new life, first step of new life, first step of new life.*

Why was it so easy for Ann and Katie?

Ann and Katie.

Ann and Katie had their homework done.

Ann and Katie could spend all day watching cartoons if they wanted.

Not Julie.

Julie had homework — and a useless newspaper clipping. Yay.

"Why, Julie, you're home early," Mrs. Drake said as she spooned scrambled eggs on to Mr. Drake's plate. Then she noticed Julie's hair "Don't you think that's a little much for an eleven-ye...?"

"Katie was practicing. I'm combing it out."

"Hey, Jules, how does a squid go to battle?"

Julie paused. "I don't know, Dad."

"Well-armed!"

"Very funny, Dad."

Julie trudged out of the room as Mr. Drake said, "Mother, where's the strawberry jam?"

She shut the door to her prison, flung the tote bag onto her bed, and dropped onto her desk chair, sticking her tongue out at the hateful schoolbooks. Then she reluctantly sharpened a yellow number two pencil and opened her math book.

Julie worked all morning. She ignored her growing headache and the gurgling in her middle until she heard a tap at the door.

"Are you awake?" Mrs. Drake asked.

"Yes, Mom."

"I called you three times. Lunch is ready."

"Be right down."

Mrs. Drake had made a hearty beef vegetable soup, homemade sourdough bread, and pineapple upside down cake for dessert. Nothing tasted good.

"Mother, may I have more bread?"

"A small slice, if you want dessert," Mrs. Drake passed him the plate. "Easy on the butter. You know what the doctor said."

"I'll be good, Mother."

Julie pushed her empty bowl away. "May I please be excused?"

Mrs. Drake looked perplexed. "No dessert?

"Maybe later."

"But you love pineapple upside down cake!"

Mr. Drake winked. "Jules, if you don't eat your portion, I just might…"

"I have a lot of homework."

As Julie left the room, she heard her mother say, "Maybe I should go to the school and talk to..."

But once inside her bedroom, Julie plopped on her bed instead of returning to her desk.

Maybe she should give up.

Maybe she really wasn't college material.

Maybe Cs were good enough for stupid girls with no future – like her.

Julie flopped against the pillows, crackling her tote bag, which reminded her, irritated her, and piqued her curiosity.

She pulled the clipping out and unfolded it.

What was this?

It wasn't The Munsonville Times, and it wasn't a regular newspaper story.

Julie rolled onto her stomach, smoothed the paper in front of her, and began to read, wondering why Mrs. Clements gave this story to her.

The story was about twelve third grade students and their essays. The students wrote about how their teacher had separated them into two groups by eye color.

The kids with brown eyes were told they were smart. They received privileges in the classroom.

The kids with blue eyes were told they were stupid. They received no privileges.

The kids wrote about how that made them feel, about how it made them behave.

Well, this had nothing to do with psychology. Stupid Mrs. Clements.

Julie sat up and started to rip the paper – and stopped. She swung her legs over the bed and read the twelve essays again. Then Julie slowly refolded the paper, thinking. Julie thought a very long time.

Was this how Julie was treating herself?

Julie kept calling herself "stupid" and acted as if she expected to fail.

Her father said their family wasn't "college material." But was that because they weren't smart enough for college?

Or was it because they just thought they weren't smart enough for college?

Julie looked around her room for a place to hide the clipping. Under her mattress was not good. Her mother flipped the mattress when she stripped and changed the beds every Monday.

Under her clothes was not good. Her mother rearranged Julie's drawers every Tuesday when she put the folded laundry away.

Mrs. Clements selected a dictionary and handed it to Julie.

"Look up 'psychology' and tell me what it says," Mrs. Clements said.

Julie opened the bottom drawer of her desk, took out the dictionary, flipped to "psychology," and then slipped the clipping beneath its pages. She replaced the book, shut the drawer, and headed for her tote bag. Better get that dirty laundry into the

chute before Mrs. Drake scolded.

For most of that day, Julie studied and re-studied. She stayed calm, collected, and focused – until dinner that night.

Mr. Drake had just said, "Mother, may I have more gravy..." when Julie slammed down her fork and shouted, "She has a name, you know!"

"Julie Elizabeth Drake!" Mrs. Drake pointed her fork at her. "You watch your mouth!"

Mr. Drake looked just as stunned. "Jules, is something wrong? Mother, did something hap..."

"ARGHH!"

Julie shoved her chair back and stomped out of the room.

CHAPTER 5: IT'S A FOOL'S DREAM

"I think she should see Dr. Rothgard," Julie heard Mrs. Drake say to Mr. Drake later when Julie left her bedroom to shower.

"Mother, it's Jules. She'll be fine. She's just at that age. Dave has a daughter who's eleven, too, and he said..."

Julie felt like slamming the bathroom door. Instead, she gripped the handle hard.

"...well, but if it continues, I'll call. Sam, did you take your medicine?"

Julie quietly shut the door and turned on the spray with a shaking hand. She angrily lathered up her hair and rinsed it under the showerhead that scarcely dripped water.

Dr. Rothgard!

All because Julie was studying hard!

All because Julie wanted to go to college!

All because Julie wanted to be a psychologist like Beverly Hartley!

All because Julie lived in Munsonville!

She scowled, lathered up a washcloth, and scrubbed her skin until it smarted.

Dr. Rothgard!

Julie's temper had only cooled slightly by the time she'd returned to her bedroom. Mrs. Drake was

sitting on Julie's desk chair. A plate of butter cookies and a glass of milk was sitting on Julie's desk.

"It's a fool's dream, Julie," Mrs. Drake said. Julie looked at the books on her desk.

"Mom, I have a lot of..."

Mrs. Drake gestured to bed number one. "Sit, Julie. This won't take long."

With a loud sigh, Julie sat. Mrs. Drake moved onto the bed next to Julie.

"Julie," Mrs. Drake said, brushing strands of wet hair off Julie's cheek. "I'm very proud of the extra effort with your studies."

"Thanks, Mom."

"But who filled your head with college?"

"Me."

"Julie..."

"Mom, what's so terrible about wanting to go to college?"

This time, Mrs. Drake sighed.

"Julie," she said very gently, "You don't have the discipline for college."

"I'm working on that, Mom. That's why I'm studying so hard."

"But you wouldn't practice your piano."

"I don't like playing the piano."

"That's my point. You have a natural talent for piano. And if you can't apply yourself to the piano, how will you consistently apply yourself to college studies, where you don't have..."

"Just say it, Mom! You think I'm stupid!"

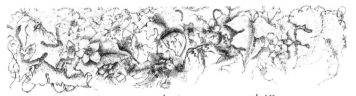

"Don't put words in my mouth!"

"You think I'm too stupid for college!"

"Julie, I'm losing my patience with you." Mrs. Drake grasped Julie's cheeks. "Now shut that fresh mouth and listen to me! You'll get sick if you keep forcing yourself to do more and more and more! And if you can't stop yourself, I'm taking you to Dr. Rothgard to find out what's wrong with you! Now eat your snack and go to bed!"

Mrs. Drake stomped out of the room and slammed the door behind her.

A lump grew in Julie's throat. Her chest felt tight. Why couldn't her parents understand? Why couldn't they help her – or at least be on her side?

Michael Morchester in "Dream Ghouls" was luckier than Julie. He had Beverly Hartley to help him. All Julie had was Dr. Rothgard, who gave out tonics. She wondered what Beverly Hartley would say if she were here now.

And then –

Beverly Hartley appeared, in a tailored suit and pilgrim pumps, sitting in Julie's desk chair, with her blonde brushed over the top of her head and holding a pen over her notebook.

Now Julie knew Beverly Hartley wasn't really sitting her chair. Julie knew she was just pretending. But even pretending was strangely comforting as Julie wrestled with herself.

"What troubles you, Julie?" Beverly Hartley asked in a kind voice.

"My mother," Julie grumbled bitterly. "My father. They think I'm too stupid for college."

"Did they say that? In actual words?"

"No," Julie admitted. "But they meant it."

Beverly Hartley tipped her head. "How do you know?"

"My mother thinks because I hate playing the piano I shouldn't go to college."

"Is she right?"

"What kind of question is that?"

"Just a question." Beverly Hartley leaned back, tapping her pen against her notebook, and looking straight sat Julie. "Is she right?"

"Why would you say that?"

"Is she?"

"No!"

"Don't you like piano music?"

"I love piano music. I hate practicing."

"But you love spending all your free time studying and working on homework?"

"No!"

"Then why give it your all?"

"You know why!"

Beverly Hartley leaned forward. "Think about it, Julie. You like the sound of piano music. But you don't like practicing to make music for yourself."

"So what?"

"So you also like the idea of becoming a psychologist. But how long will you give your all

classwork when you don't like that, either?"

"It's different!"

"How?"

Julie heard a knock on the door. Beverly Hartley vanished.

"Julie," Mrs. Drake said from the other side. "Have you eaten your snack?"

"Soon, Mom."

"Well, hurry up. I want to finish the dishes."

"Sure, Mom."

Slowly, Julie got up and slowly walked to her desk. She picked up a cookie and nibbled around its edge, thinking.

She sank into her desk chair, still thinking about Beverly Hartley's words, which were really Julie's words, when Julie pretended Beverly Hartley was sitting in her room.

Was that why Mrs. Drake meant about Julie not having the discipline for college? Would Julie only go so far and give up? Was her dream weaker than her drive?

Julie reached for her milk.

She pictured it again: *Julie Drake, psychologist* on a gold nameplate.

"It's not a fool's dream," Julie said aloud.

Then prove it, Beverly Hartley answered from somewhere in the back of Julie's mind.

"I will!" Julie exclaimed.

She raised her glass of milk. "To me – and my future!"

Then Julie drained the glass and started making those cookies disappear, too.

CHAPTER: 6: THE PAPER THAT CHANGED
EVERYTHING

On Saturday morning, Julie was plodding through area and perimeter when she heard a knock at the front door.

A few moments later Ann and Katie appeared in her doorway, holding their plastic tote bags.

"Let us in," Ann said.

"Why?"

Katie giggled. "Silly. To do homework together."

Julie sighed and rolled her eyes. But she stepped aside to let the girls enter.

"We know you're really smart, and you work really hard," Ann said after Julie shut the bedroom door. "So Katie and I talked about it. We want to help you get done sooner."

Katie nodded. "Ann asked me how I did my homework. And then she told me how she does hers. And guess what?"

"I give up."

"We do homework differently!"

Julie shrugged. "So what?"

Ann sat on the edge of bed number one. "Well, what if you tried doing your homework differently?"

"What do you mean by 'differently?'" Julie turned in her chair to face Ann. "There's only one

way to do homework."

Katie plopped onto bed number two. Mittens and Muffy jumped of and ran under the bed. "That's not true! That's why we're here. Ann thought if we did homework together, you might get ideas."

"What sort of ideas?"

Ann took out a notebook and pencil and started to write. Katie took her school supplies out of her tote bag and laid them across Julie's bed.

"What are you doing?" Julie asked.

"I'm making a list," Ann said.

"What kind of list?"

Ann held up her notebook. "I'm writing down everything I have to do."

"What are those numbers?"

"It's how long I think it will take," Ann said.

"With breaks," Katie added.

Julie blinked. "Breaks?"

"You don't take breaks?" Katie asked.

"How can I take breaks?" Julie angrily blew her braids off her face. "If I took breaks, I'd never get done!" She looked at the papers and books on bed number two. "What are you doing?"

"Making piles."

"I can see that!"

"I'm getting the easy homework out of the way first," Katie said. "I can focus on the hardest homework."

"Not me," Ann chimed in. "I'm get the hard homework done first before I'm tired. Then I fly

through the easy homework." She glanced at her watch. "First break is in fifteen minutes."

"Ready, set – go!" Katie shouted.

"Wait!" Julie held up her hand. "Should I choose something hard or easy?"

Ann shrugged and opened her math book. Katie was already lying on her stomach, kicking her legs in the air, scribbling out her spelling words.

Julie signed, turned around, and returned to calculating the perimeter of an acute triangle.

"Break time!" Katie shrieked.

Julie covered her ear with one hand and whirled around. "Break time?"

Ann was already on her feet and stretching,

Katie bounded off the bed and out the door into the bathroom.

"It's just a short break." Ann put her hands on her hips and leaned from side to side. "Mom said a good stretch gets blood flowing to the brain."

Julie made a face and threw down her pencil. But she stood and half-heartedly raised her hands to the ceiling. Might as well, she thought. She'd tried everything else.

"Hurray!" Katie cried as she ran back in. "You're doing it!"

"Break's over," Ann announced.

Julie stopped in mid-stretch. "Already?"

"It's just a short break," Katie said.

Julie plopped onto her desk chair and grabbed her pencil, and muttered, "Too short,"

under her breath.

All that afternoon, the girls worked in fifteen-minute increments, pausing to stretch or do thirty jumping jacks, grab a glass of water and pet Mittens and Muffy, who decided to share the bed with Katie after all. They sipped cold glasses of milk and munched still-warm sugar cookies from Mrs. Drake that everyone enjoyed, even Julie.

Ann and Katie finished all their homework in two hours and left shortly before dinner, praising Julie for her progress. Julie, of course, wasn't done. But she only had her spelling words to copy and reading questions to tackle. And her head had stopped hurting.

Julie flew through the rest of her homework after dinner that night. On Sunday morning after church, she helped her dad wash the car. After lunch, she took a long bike ride with Ann and Katie. She felt as free as the wind rippling through her braids now that she'd solved the dilemma of the everlasting homework. One problem conquered!

But Julie's doubts returned on Monday. She struggled with converting decimals to percentages in class and then she struggled to remember the steps later that afternoon at her desk. Julie tried not think about the other assignments waiting for her – worksheets on direct and indirect objects, an essay on the principal products of Sweden, and her new vocabulary and spelling list.

"I get the hard homework done first before I'm tired. Then I fly through the easy homework."

Maybe math wasn't the best first choice, Julie thought with a surge of panic at the temptation of leaving it for last. She saw herself drowsing over her math book at midnight – and panic flared again.

"What are you doing?"
"I'm making a list."

Slowly, Julie opened her notebook. She glanced at the pile of books to her right. Copying her spelling was easy, Julie thought as she wrote spelling at the top of the page, and not that time-consuming, maybe fifteen minutes. Vocabulary wasn't too bad, either. Julie only had to write a sentence for each word. If Julie didn't know the meaning, she could quickly open her dictionary and find it.

That should take another fifteen minutes, maybe twenty, Julie thought, writing that down, too.

She could pause at that point and head down to the kitchen for milk and cookies. Wouldn't Mrs. Drake be surprised!

Mrs. Drake *was* surprised – but Julie even more so. Julie finished her homework, all of it, even math, in enough time to join her parents for ten minutes in their latest puzzle, a snow-capped

mountain scene.

A week later, Julie received her quarterly report card. The days before THAT day were the worst days in Julie's whole life. She'd worked so hard. What if she still only made Cs – or worse

She woke with a headache and a stomachache every day. She could scarcely eat or drink or concentrate on her assignments. Her hands shook when she wrote or picked up a pencil. Worse, she had nightmares every night on the scale of "Dream Ghouls" which destroyed any chance of restful sleep.

On THAT day, Julie plodded down Bass Street, with her stomach flip-flopping under a heavy weight of thick oatmeal. At the bottom of the hill, she forced her reluctant feet every inch of the way.

Julie paused outside that three-story red brick building and gazed at the students of all ages and sizes climbing the steps and passing through the front doors.

"What if you tried doing your homework differently?"

This was the real test. And Julie was terrified she wouldn't pass it.

WHAT IF anything Julie tried didn't matter?
WHAT IF she'd failed again?
Julie felt a slap on her shoulder and turned to see Katie zipping past, waving her hand. Well, Julie

couldn't stay out here all day. She dragged herself up the steps and through the door.

Naturally, Mrs. Fitzgerald waited until the end of the school day to pass out the first quarter report cards.

Mrs. Fitzgerald was the new fifth and sixth grade teacher, a friend of Katie's brothers, so she had "the look" of someone outside Munsonville. Her brown hair was combed over her head and held in place with a silver headband. She wore cat-eyeglasses with sparkling gems in the pointy corners. And she wore pink lipstick and transparent pink nail polish, the only woman Julie ever met up close that looked so sophisticated.

Julie's heart raced as Mrs. Fitzgerald slowly walked up and down the few short rows of desks and set report cards face down on each student's desk. It didn't take long; the combined fifth and sixth grades only had seventeen students.

With her heart pounding loudly in her ears, Julie watched each student lift the report card by a corner and slowly turn it over.

Bobby Brown's face puckered under his thick tousle of hair, but he didn't cry.

Dan Walker guffawed and ran his hand through his red crew cut.

Katie breathed out a huge sigh.

Ann, as well as Jack Cooper, simply slid their report cards into their tote bags. But then, homework came easy for Ann and Jack. They never

earned anything but As.

Mrs. Fitzgerald set Julie report card on her desk and kept walking. Julie wiped her sweating palms across her plaid skirt and gingerly picked up the scary paper by one corner. She held her breath – and then quickly flipped it over.

B-

Julie's eyes filled with tears.

For the first time in her whole entire life, she averaged a B- for all her classes.

Julie quickly wiped her eyes.

Ann, of course, had straight As. Katie had a mix of As and Bs. Julie didn't have a single A.

For the first time, Julie didn't care.

For the first time, Julie had something better than As on her report card.

And Julie felt that "something better" for a long time even as she stared at that B- for a long time and took her time walking home, tears of relief and joy streaking her cheeks.

Because for the first time Julie had encouragement – and hope – that she was on the right track to a bright and marvelous future.

And that was all because of a little piece of paper with a B- written on it with red ink.

And – boy! Did it feel good!

CHAPTER 7: TIME TO WAKE UP

Mrs. Drake was so pleased with Julie's report card that she let Julie go fishing with Dr. Drake early Saturday morning, even though Julie hadn't quite finished all her homework on Friday night.

Here's how it happened.

Mr. Drake barely noticed when Mrs. Drake handed him that wonderful piece of paper. But Mr. Drake also looked distracted, so Julie forgave him for scarcely noticing. He didn't tell one joke at dinner or during the cribbage game Julie played with her parents that night.

But as he and Julie picked up the pieces and set them back into the box, he abruptly said, "Mother, I feel like the fish will bite tomorrow morning. Can Julie go with me – if she promises to hit the books as soon as we come home?"

Mrs. Drake raised her eyebrows at this lapse in her rules. Then she smiled. "I think that would be fine. Julie has worked very hard. A little reward is in order. I will pack a breakfast.

Julie's heart sank as she trudged up the stairs. She had planned to finish her homework first thing in the morning. She and Ann were meeting at Katie's house that afternoon to work on their Halloween costumes. Katie's Mom had an old sewing machine and always made their costumes. Maybe Mr. Drake would quickly catch a lot of fish. Maybe Julie, if she hurried, would finish before lunchtime.

But probably not, Julie thought with a sinking heart. Halloween was two weeks away. How would she ever get a good costume now?

BRRRIIINGGGG! BRINNNGGG!

"Mrumph!"

Julie clambered to her knees, fumbling in the dark for her alarm clock – *BLINGGgunginginging!*

The clock bounced onto the floor and went silent.

With a loud, frustrated sigh, Julie untwisted herself from the coil of covers and leaned over the side of her head, swiping her hand here and there.

Nothing.

She groped for a dresser drawer, pulled it out, and then felt around for her flashlight – got it! Julie switched it on, blinked against the brightness and shone the beam around the room.

Nothing.

She groaned, loudly this time as she slid off the bed and onto her knees. There it was, under her bed, just out of reach. She stretched and wiggled her fingers, but Julie only grazed its face. Finally, she stood up, pulled the bed back, and picked it up. Five minutes after four o'clock, ugh!

Every limb ached. Her sleepy mind felt stuffed with cotton and half-dreams. Julie padded to the door and cracked it open, hoping her father had changed his mind.

But no, Julie heard faint kitchen sounds. She glanced at her rumpled bed, which never had looked cozier.

"Julie," Mrs. Drake said very gently, "You don't have the discipline for college...if you can't apply yourself to fishing, how will you consistently apply yourself to college studies?"

Julie thought of all the times in "Dream Ghouls" that Michael Morchester called Beverly Hartley in the middle of the night because he had no one else to help him. Each time, Beverly Hartley had left her bed and met him at her office, perfectly groomed and poised. *Julie Drake, psychologist.*

Yawning loudly, Julie stumbled to her dresser.

Ten minutes later, Julie's feet were lightly tapping on the wooden stairs. She saw the light spilling from the kitchen doorway.

Mr. Drake snapped his large metal lunchbox shut as Julie stumbled into the room, and the snap sounded like a firecracker in the silent house.

"Morning, Dad," Julie mumbled.

Mr. Drake beamed. "Morning, Jules. Ready to wake up the walleyes?"

She yawned behind her hand. "Sure Dad."

"You take the thermoses."

Julie nodded. She always took the thermoses.

Mr. Drake switched the light off as she

opened the screen door and stepped into the misty dark. She heard clink of Mr. Drake's keys behind her. She waited on the stoop with the lunch box while Mr. Drake went into the garage for his tackle box, nightcrawlers from the worm bin, and two fishing poles.

The misty dark always reminded Julie of Munsonville's ghost legend. On mornings like today Julie almost wished the legend were true. A ghost would be exciting. But nothing exciting ever happened in Munsonville. Not even a dream ghoul showed its spooky face.

Mr. Drake locked the garage's side door and turned to Julie. "Ready, Jules?"

"Sure, Dad."

They walked down Bass Street, with Julie holding a thermos in each hand and her father holding the rest, including a flashlight. The metal handles burned her fingers. Julie didn't talk. Mr. Drake didn't talk. Mr. Drake always said early morning wasn't made for talking.

Slowly they followed the beam of light. They carefully crossed an empty Main Street. Their shoes squeaked on the wet grass as they passed the fishing cabins. Finally, they reached the dock. Their footsteps rumbled loudly on the old boards all the way to the edge. Julie set the thermoses near the lunch box and waved her smarting hands in the cold air. Then she dropped cross-legged onto the dock and gazed across the rolling black waters.

While Mr. Drake baited the hooks, Julie watched the waves rush to the dock. Did big cities have lakes, she wondered.

Mr. Drake handed Julie a pole.

They sat quietly, holding their rods in one hand and munching peanut butter and apple sandwiches from the other. Mr. Drake held Julie's pole while she poured steaming hot coffee for him and hot chocolate for her into the plastic thermos caps. They still didn't talk. Mr. Drake always said chatter chased the fish away.

So that's why Julie jumped when he broke the silence. "I'm proud of your report card, Jules."

A feeling warmer than hot chocolate flowed through Julie, and she wriggled like a fish on a hook.

"Thanks, Dad. I worked really hard."

"I know."

"I have a goal."

"College. I know."

They fished in silence for a long time. Then Mr. Drake, peering into the water, said softly, "It's time to wake up."

Julie giggled. Mr. Drake never talked to fish.

"The walleye sure are sleepy today, Dad."

Mr. Drake looked sternly at Julie. "I'm not talking to the fish. I'm talking to you."

"Huh? But I am..."

"Wake up from your college dream."

"No!"

Mr. Drake blinked and recoiled. Julie

trembled inside her coat, waiting for the smack across her mouth. Her parents didn't tolerate backtalk.

But Mr. Drake only looked at the waves, hanging his head. The night was fading to a pink-steaked day.

"We can't afford college, Jules" Mr. Drake said bluntly, with shame in his voice. "It costs money, lots of money."

"But Dad!" Julie's heart pounded hard and fast. "If I work super hard, I can get scholarships. Mrs. Clements said that..."

"Do you know how many scholarships you'll need to pay for college? How will you find them all? How will you qualify for that many?"

Mr. Drake's words sucked the breath out of Julie. The lake swam before her eyes. Why wasn't he taking her dream seriously?

"That's why I'm starting now to improve my grades. That's why..."

"You'll never improve them to the extent of covering college tuition."

Mr. Drake's voice trembled a little. Julie, already reeling with anger and disappointed that her own father had basically called her stupid, almost gasped aloud at his tremble. Mr. Drake was happy-go-lucky and upbeat. His voice never trembled.

He's upset, Julie suddenly realized. He's upset because he's my dad, and he can't make my

dream come true.

Pale yellow rays glinted off the Lake Munson. She suddenly felt so grownup, she almost hugged Mr. Drake, but she didn't, just in case a fish was getting ready to nibble.

Instead she said, "Then I'll find another way, Dad. You'll see."

Mr. Drake brushed a sleeve across his face and turned to Julie with a weak smile.

"Munsonville's is a wonderful place to raise a family. "My Jules is a mart girl. You'll make a great mom."

CHAPTER 8: WHAT'S A PIANO GOT TO DO WITH IT?

Neither Katie nor Julie's family had telephones, so Julie had no way to tell them she couldn't come over on Saturday. She had no way to tell them that Mr. Drake had decided to take her fishing at the last minute, and that she still had homework to complete.

That detail worked in Julie's favor.

Torn between Julie's two obligations, Mrs. Drake decided Julie should not desert her friends nor disrespect Mrs. Miller's time.

"But you must go straight to your room when you return home," Mrs. Drake said as she stacked the last lunch plate in the drying rack. "No other amusements until your schoolwork is done."

"I know, Mom." Julie leaned up to kiss her cheek. "I only have math left."

Julie softly shut the door behind her and trudged up Bass Street, yawning every few steps.

After their short fishing trip, where even Mr. Drake, an expert fisherman, didn't catch one fish, Julie had dutifully climbed the stairs to her room and opened her books.

For three hours, Julie stoically fought the urge to jump back into bed. When sleep waves washed over her and blurred the words on the page, Julie gripped her pencil tighter or threw it down in

favor of stretches and jumping jacks.

But now, after a satisfying soup and sandwich lunch, and walking outside in the warm autumn sunshine and the brisk air, Julie sank into drowsiness; each step up the steep hill took more and more effort. Still, a happy little flame burned inside Julie. She had learned new ways to study; she had earned a B-. So how hard could finding college scholarships be?

Julie Drake, psychologist...

At the top of the hill, she cut across the side yard of the last house over to the top of Blue Gill Road and Katie's house.

"Hi, Julie!" Katie cried when she opened the front door. "We're just getting started."

Mrs. Miller, a tall, broad-shouldered, muscular woman with tightly knotted yellow bun hinting of gray, was sitting at the treadle sewing machine in Katie's living room, steadily pumping pedal and moving the needle through the shimmery white fabric. Julie smelled buttery popcorn.

"Whose costume?" Julie asked.

"Mine," Ann said, walking from the kitchen with a huge bowl of popped corn and a handful of paper napkins. "I'm a ghost."

Katie shuddered. "She wants to shimmer in the dark." Then she grinned. "I can't wait to see it!"

Ann grabbed a handful of popcorn and set

the bowl and napkins on the table next to stacks of fabric remnants and old clothes.

"My mom said she'd give us masks from the store," Ann said. "Because Mrs. Miller is making the costumes for us."

Ann's parents ran Dalton's Dry Goods on Main Street. They carried a few essential Halloween items, including witch hats and vampire teeth.

Mrs. Miller glanced up from the sewing machine with a smile.

"Pick something, Julie." Katie said excitedly.

Julie glanced at dizzying cluster of stripes and plaids, solid pastels and bolds, and satin, corduroy, polyester, and cotton. She stifled a yawn as she asked, "What's your costume, Katie?"

Katie pointed to an old black velvet evening gown on the chair next to Mrs. Miller. "A witch. And Mom's making me a cape from old curtains."

"Black curtains?" Julie asked doubtfully.

Mrs. Miller laughed over the rumble of the sewing machine. "They will be after I dye them."

"They're beige right now," Katie said around a mouthful of popcorn. "And full of stains from my brothers when they were little. She's adding a satin back. So even if it's cold, I'll be warm. Mrs. Dalton already set my hat aside." She grinned at Mrs. Miller. "I'll match Mommy this year."

In Munsonville, Halloween wasn't just for children. Everyone dressed up, even the grownups who passed out the candy. Mrs. Miller always

dressed as a witch.

"What do you want to be, Julie?" Ann asked.

Asleep, Julie thought as she willed back another yawn. She sank to the floor in front of table, happy to be off her feet. She sorted through the piles, hoping an idea might leap out.

"How about a clown?" Ann asked.

Julie looked up. Ann was holding a pair of polka dot pajamas.

"Yes!" Katie ran to her mother's large workbasket and held up two skeins of yard. "We can make pom poms and sew them on. And we can make a yarn wig from old tights."

"Sure," Julie said, reaching out her hand. Ann passed the popcorn bowl.

On Monday after school, Julie begged off a costume fitting at Katie's in favor of the library, insisting her books were due.

"We'll wait for you," Katie said.

Julie shook her head. "I...I need to look for...for something. I don't want to make you late."

"Just come afterwards," Ann said.

"Not this time. Mom's bent the rules a lot for me this weekend.

"Tomorrow?" Katie asked hopefully.

"I'll ask Mom and let you know at school."

"OK." Katie sounded disappointment.

Ann and Katie headed in the direction of the hill and Blue Gill Road. Julie turned right on Main Street toward the library, thinking deeply about

college scholarships. Maybe the library had a book, or a magazine or a catalogue that listed them all.

For half an hour, Julie wandered aimlessly up and down the aisles, scanning rows of titles, and finding nothing about scholarships. What good was a library if you can't find what you need, Julie thought impatiently.

She rounded the corner and almost bumped in Mrs. Clements.

"Sorry, Mrs. Clements," Julie mumbled and started to walk away when Mrs. Clements said, "Julie, did you read the newspaper article?"

Julie nodded.

"Was it helpful?"

Julie nodded again.

"But?"

Julie shrugged and looked away, wishing she could run away.

"Julie, what's wrong?"

She looked up. "My parents can't afford college. And I don't know where to find scholarships."

"I see."

"And my dad said I'll never find enough to pay for college."

Mrs. Clements frowned. "Julie, meet me at one of the tables. I want to show you something."

Julie glanced back at the wall clock. It was nearly four. Mrs. Drake served dinner at six sharp.

She stifled a sigh and headed to a table. She

was in no mood for a lecture. She dropped into a chair, setting her tote bag at her feet. Mrs. Clement was walking briskly to the table holding a folder and smiling.

"I just received it today," Mrs. Clements said as she sat beside Julie. "I sent for it the day you shared your goal of becoming a psychologist."

Julie remembered. The day Mrs. Clements had given her the newspaper clipping.

"You've heard of John Simons, the famous piano player who lived Munsonville almost a century ago, haven't you?"

Julie nodded. Everyone in Munsonville knew about John Simons.

Mrs. Clements opened the folder and moved it close to Julie.

"Well, dear, before John Simons died in 1955, he left an endowment to Jenson College. Do you know what an endowment is?"

Julie shook her head.

"Basically, John Simons left part of his fortune to Jenson College to pay the full amount of certain students' tuition."

Julie's heart skipped a beat. She sat up straight. "The full amount? All of it?"

Mrs. Clements nodded happily. "Yes, all of it. However, John Simons had one condition."

"What's that?" Julie asked breathlessly, disbelieving her ears and her good fortune.

"The money is only given to accomplished

piano students."

Julie's stomach dropped. "What???"

Her eyes burned. Her throat felt too tight to swallow. She could scarcely breathe.

"But Mrs. Clements," Julie whispered. "I don't want to study..."

"That's the best part, Julie. John Simons didn't require the student to major in piano to receive the scholarship. The student must simply be accomplished on piano. Isn't that wonderful?"

"I hate playing the piano," Julie spat out, not caring if she sounded disrespectful or not.

"Julie, I...I don't understand. Aren't you still taking lessons from your mother? You sounded quite good at last year's talent show."

"I stopped."

The smile faded from Mrs. Clements' face. "Oh. I see. Well, maybe this will motivate you to..."

"Why is this my problem?" Julie burst out. "This should be my parents' problem. I studied really, really hard and got my grades up. I did my part. But Mom and Dad aren't happy for me. They won't help me. They won't even try to figure out how to pay for college."

"Julie..."

"I hate piano!"

Mrs. Clements closed the folder and picked it up. She slid back her chair. But she did not stand, not just yet.

"Julie," she said softly. "You are very

mistaken. The list of things parents must do for their children is really quite short. No one simply hands you anything, not even a scholarship. You must work for it."

Julie angrily blew a stray hair off her face. "But I AM working for it. I study and study and study and study. And I'm not THAT good on piano, even if I liked it. It's hopeless."

She swiped hot tears off her face and grabbed her bag. Mrs. Clements laid a hand on Julie shoulder. In Julie's mind, every library patron was staring at her.

"It's not hopeless," Mrs. Clements said. "Did you know Michigan State University created the first program in music therapy? Yes, right here in Michigan."

"Music therapy?" Julie asked scornfully when she really wanted to scream. "What's music therapy?"

"Talk therapy, where clients talk about their problems to their psychologist, is just one type of therapy. Music therapy, where music is incorporated into a patient's healing, is another."

"But Beverly Hartley..." Julie blurted out than clapped a hand to her mouth.

Mrs. Clements looked confused. "Whose Beverly Hartley?"

"No one," Julie mumbled, mortified that she'd let that slip. She closed her eyes and let Mrs. Clements drone on. Today was the worst day of her

whole life.

"Your piano training might become part of your psychology practice. Don't shut a door on an opportunity just because you assume what's behind it. A wise girl shoots many arrows at the target. Open the door and explore."

Julie opened her eyes and glared at Mrs. Clements. *"I hate piano."*

"So learn to like it," Mrs. Clements said. "That puts four years of paid college into your lap. You don't have to be Mozart, just persistent about improving. And if you're serious about it," Mrs. Clements added as she rose, "Jenson College has a new music professor that's accepting a few private students. Maybe you can look into that. Oh, and you will need to pay for the lessons. Now, if you're interested, I need someone to shelve books after school and on Saturday afternoon. Let me know."

Julie snatched her bag and ran out of the library, crying hard now as she stomped up the hill. Now the whole world knew. *Julie Drake, psychologist.* What an idiot she was! She picked out the right Halloween costume all right! Her door tag should read *Julie Drake, clown.*

She flew through the front door, sticking her tongue at the silent piano, just sitting in the front window, mocking her. Then she ran up the stairs two at a time and nearly slammed her bedroom door.

Piano! Ugh!

Julie flung her tote bag on her end and flopped onto her desk chair, automatically reaching for a pencil and pencil sharpener. Then she slammed them both down on her desk. She didn't need to work so hard anymore, not if she was just going to get married and have babies. Julie's hard work was for nothing. What difference did a B- make now?

But Julie's new habits were now part of her, like skin; they resisted shedding. One by one, Julie snatched her books from her tote bag. She scrawled out a list of assignments; she started copying her spelling words. Her fingers tightly gripped the pencil and pressed so hard onto the paper her fingers hurt.

Snatches of conversation burst into Julie's thoughts like sparks from a bonfire.

"You have a natural talent for piano. And if you can't apply yourself to the piano, how will you consistently apply yourself to college studies..."

"Just say it, Mom! You think I'm stupid!"

"No one simply hands you anything, not even a scholarship. You must work for it."

"I hate piano."

"So learn to like it. That puts four years of paid college into your lap."

Julie groaned but kept writing. Why did it have to be piano? She hated the pointless repetition of it. Plunk, plunk, plunk, plink, plunk, plink, plonk, plunk, plunk.

She felt like crying.

She kept on writing.

Julie slept restlessly that night and woke up with her nose stuffy, her face wet, her damp pajamas clinging to her skin, and the crampiest stomachache in her life. She shook while getting dressed and braided her hair and tied her shoelaces with stiff, clumsy fingers.

But she stunned Mr. and Mrs. Drake at the breakfast table when she announced in a loud voice, "I want to take piano lessons."

CHAPTER 9: A BIT FROM ME, A BIT FROM YOU

"Piano lessons!" Mrs. Drake exclaimed. "What brought this on?"

"College," Julie said firmly as she buttered her toast.

Mr. and Mrs. Drake exchanged nervous glances.

"Julie," Mrs. Drake said gently. "If this is about our conversation the other day..."

"It's about a scholarship at Jenson College," Julie said, setting down her knife and looking from one parent to the next. "Mrs. Clements said John Simons left an endo...an endo...some money to pay the tuition for really good piano students. Dad said he can't afford college. So I will earn it myself."

Julie picked up her toast and took a bite. Mr. Drakes' cheeks turned bright pink.

"Jules," he said in a husky voice. He cleared his throat. "Jules, you aren't...fond...of piano. You spend so much time studying. I, er, your mother and I...we'd rather..."

"Dad, I've made up my mind. I'm going to take piano lessons."

"Julie," Mrs. Drake tried again. "Of course, I'm thrilled you want to take lessons. But learning to play the piano is more than weekly lessons. It's..."

"I know, Mom. It's daily practice." Julie

stuffed the last bite of toast into her mouth. "And I'm ready to start when you are. Because I'm also working on a second goal."

Mr. Drake and Mrs. Drake looked at each other again, really bewildered now.

"Goal?" Mr. Drake asked in a quivering voice.

"Yes. Mrs. Clements said Jenson College has a new music professor who gives private lessons. I want to get good enough to take lessons from him."

Mr. Drake turned pale. "Julie, you can't take lessons at Jenson College for…"

"For free, Dad. I know. I'll need a job."

Mrs. Drake leaped to her feet. "Julie, I don't know what's gotten into you! A job? At eleven! When you struggle with school! Just where will you get a job?"

Julie took a sip of milk. "Jack Cooper's eleven and he helps at Sue's Diner."

"That's different, Jules. His parents own Sue's Diner."

"Ann helps out at Dalton's Dry Goods."

Mrs. Drake shoved her chair against table so hard the dishes rattled. "Julie, knock it off! You know very well Ann's parents own the dry goods store."

After a very loud AHEM, Mr. Drake said, "I don't suppose, Julie Girl, you'll be asking me…"

"No, Dad. I'm not asking for a job at the used car lot. Mrs. Clements offered me a job shelving books at the library."

Mr. Drake breathed a loud sigh of relief. Mrs. Drake started collecting the dishes with loud clatters. Her lips were tightly pursed. Parents!

Suddenly, Mrs. Drake dropped back into her chair. She looked hard at Julie.

"Julie, are you serious about making this commitment?"

"Yes, Mom. I'm very serious."

"Then you will need a budget."

"A budget?"

"Yes. A budget. You will need to find out what lessons cost, what transportation to and from Jenson costs, what you need to earn, and how many hours you will need to work to earn it."

"OK."

But Julie didn't feel OK. She cringed at "transportation" and "cost." She'd assumed her parents would drive her. But then she quickly remembered Mrs. Clements' words: "No one simply hands you anything, not even a scholarship. You must work for it." Right there, Julie made up her mind to be grown up about it, like Beverly Hartley.

"It's almost the end of October. If, and this is a big if, Julie. IF you get the job, and IF you can afford to pay for piano lessons, and IF you keep your grades up, and IF you take lessons with me seriously, THEN and ONLY THEN, will I allow you to apply for piano lessons at Jenson College in the spring.

Julie leaped out of her chair and flung her

arms around her mother's neck, kissing her cheek over and over and over again.

"Thank you! Thank you!" Julie cried. "You are the best mom ever!"

"Hey, Jules!" Mr. Drake cried. "What's a cow's favorite day at school?"

"I give up, Dad."

"When it goes on a field trip!" Mr. Drake burst out laughing at his joke. "Get it?"

"Got it, Dad. May I pleased be excused?"

Mr. Drake pointed at the door. "Yes. Go."

As Julie left the room to brush her teeth, she heard her father say, "Mother, I think we raised a future college student."

Julie grinned all the way up the stairs.

At lunch that day, Katie reminded Julie that she had promised to try on her costume that day, in case Mrs. Miller needed to make any adjustments.

Julie gulped. She had forgotten.

"I...I can still make it," Julie stammered. "But I have to stop at the library first."

"Again?" Ann bit into a crisp apple. "Why?"

Katie giggled. "Did you read ALL your books? Already?"

"I have to talk to Mrs. Clements about...about something. And then I have to stop at home and tell Mom I'm going to your house. I forgot this morning."

"We'll walk with you," Ann said in a decided, matter-of-fact voice.

"Um, that's not nec..."

Ann turned to Julie. "If your Mom says, 'No,' how will we know?"

Julie thought about it. "OK, you can walk with me."

"If she says, 'No,' I'll fall on my knees and beg!" Katie exclaimed, clasping her hands, and gazing at the ceiling in mock rapture.

Julie laughed and milk ran out her nose. She grabbed a paper napkin. "I'm sure Mom will let me. But it's good to be sure."

To the awe of Ann and Katie, Mrs. Clements waved Julie over to the front desk and immediately confirmed Julie had the job.

"You may start tomorrow," Mrs. Clements said. "You'll have some forms to fill out first."

For once, Katie the chatterbox had nothing to say as the girls walked up Blue Gill Road. Ann, who was naturally quiet, kicked a stone through the leaves for most of the way with her head down, obviously in deep thought.

Abruptly, Katie stopped in the middle of the street and wailed, "We hardly see you anymore! And now you've got a job! Why?"

Julie took a deep breath. "It's a long story. But I have a goal."

Katie grabbed Julie's arm. "Do you hate us?"

"No!"

"I think you're mean, mean, mean!"

Katie broke into a run. Julie's mouth

dropped, confused.

Ann linked her arm into Julie's and pulled her forward. "Don't mind Katie. I'm happy for you. What's your goal?"

"College."

It sounded flat to Julie's ears, just the way she felt.

Ann stopped. "College?" Her eyes looked intense behind the black rims of her glasses.

"Yes. Remember when we saw 'Dream Ghouls?'"

Ann nodded. "I remember."

"My favorite part was Beverly Hartley."

"The psychologist?"

"Yes. I want to be one like her."

"Oh."

They resumed their walk, neither speaking. As they neared Katie's house, Ann said, "I'm glad."

"Glad? For what?"

"For you. For working so hard to make your dream come true."

Julie's heart jumped into her throat. "Really, Ann? Truly?"

"Yes. Really, truly. And ignore Katie for now. She'll come around."

"You're sure?"

"Certain sure."

Arm in arm, the girls walked the rest of the way to Katie's, ready to spend the rest of the afternoon as a clown, a ghost, and a witch.

But that was OK with Julie.

CHAPTER 10: PRACTICE, PRACTICE, PRACTICE

The next few months passed in a blur as Julie adjusted to her new routine, feeling like she'd hopped onto an everlasting merry-go-round.

Julie spent the first hour after every school day working at the library, shelving cart after cart of books and periodicals.

Once Julie arrived home, she was expected to practice piano for another hour or until dinner was ready, whichever came first.

After dinner, Julie still had to tackle her homework. More than once, Julie fell asleep on her books, and Mrs. Drake had to help her to bed number one and slide off Julie's shoes.

But Julie's merry-go-around didn't slow down on weekends.

Right after breakfast on Saturday mornings, Julie obediently sat on the piano bench with Mrs. Drake for a two-hour piano lesson, the most dreaded part of Julie's week.

Mrs. Drake played well and expected the same from Julie. But Julie's fingers were short and clumsy. Julie struggled with chords and striking the right notes at the right time. When Julie was younger, Mrs. Drake used to scold Julie for her mistakes. She didn't scold now, but Mrs. Drake showed her disappointment in her heavy sighs and

pursed lips. More than once during Julie's practice sessions, while Mrs. Drake was cooking dinner, silent tears fell from Julie's eyes and onto the hateful keys. But Julie didn't complain out loud. Mrs. Drake had made it clear from the beginning that Jenson College piano teachers wouldn't accept just any students. If Julie wanted to qualify, she must prove her skill. But no amount of practicing was improving Julie's skill as far she could see. The sounds Julie plunked out made even Julie cringe. She despaired at ever making anything close to music. Every time she felt tempted to qui, she saw the words *Julie Drake, psychologist* in her mind. So Julie slogged on.

Besides, Mrs. Drake was charging Julie two dollars per lesson. Julie had to pay Mrs. Drake the two dollars before the lesson started. Julie worked too hard to earn that money. No way would Julie waste it!

Then right after lunch on Saturday afternoons, Julie trudged down the hill to Munsonville Library, past small children playing tag in their yards or Ann and Katie whizzing past her on their bikes. Julie shelved book after book after book until closing time, when she dragged her tired body up the hill to dinner. Mrs. Clements paid Julie nine dollars a week from her petty cash fund for nine hours of work – with an extra bonus dollar if Julie didn't miss a day of work. And Julie never did.

Right after dinner on Saturday evenings, Julie tackled more homework. More than once, Julie

fell asleep on her books, and Mrs. Drake had to help her to bed and slide off Julie's shoes.

On Sunday mornings, Julie walked to Munsonville Congregational Church for services.

On Sunday afternoon, Julie grabbed her tote bag full of books and headed to Katie's or Ann's house to work on homework together. For Ann and Katie now saved some of their work for Sunday afternoons, so they could spend that time with Julie. As Ann had promised, Katie finally did "come around."

But Katie didn't "come around" until after the big fight on Halloween night.

Ann and Katie had walked to Julie's house after school on Friday, carrying large brown paper shopping bags. The bags held their pajamas, costumes, clothes for Saturday, and their toothbrushes, for they were spending the night in Julie's room and had great plans. Ann also brought the promised masks from Dalton's Dry Goods, carefully wrapped in tissues paper so they wouldn't get crushed.

After a quick and early supper of grilled cheese sandwiches and vegetable soup, served by Mrs. Drake in cat print pajamas, the girls trooped upstairs to change.

Ann's ghost costume, made from an old white, shimmery evening gown, was the prettiest of the costumes. Mrs. Miller had cut away the extra fabric to sew a hooded cowl that slipped over it. Ann

swept up her shoulder-length chestnut hair with metal hair clips and bobby pins to hide all the strands. She only wore a black plastic half mask because of her glasses.

"But I don't mind," Ann said, smiling mysteriously.

Katie looked sweetly witchy in her repurposed curtains, an old wig from her grandmother that Mrs. Miller dyed black, and the witch hat Mrs. Dalton had set aside in Dalton's Dry Goods for her.

"Hehehehehhe," Katie cackled to her reflection in the mirror as she raised clawed fingers.

Julie watched the fun as she slid on the old polka dot pajamas from one of Katie's brothers. The large red pom poms that Mrs. Miller had wrapped from yarn bounced as she dressed. Normally Julie loved Halloween: the chilly night air with the faint scent of bonfires and costumed characters parading the streets and clambering up front steps to lighted doors guarded by grinning jack-o-lanterns. Julie loved scuffling through the leaves with her friends. She loved lifting her scratchy mask from her sweaty face to munch sweet popcorn balls or taffy apples, biting past the sticky caramel into the fruit's tart, crisp flesh.

But tonight, Julie was so exhausted, even getting dressed was too much effort.

"Here's your mask." Ann handed Julie a white mask with a painted red mouth, eyes, and

nose. "And here's yours." Ann gave Katie a green witch mask with a molded nose and blackened teeth.

Katie put on her mask and spun around.

"Hehehehehhe," Katie cackled to her friends.

"Boo!" Ann retorted.

Julie pulled the old tights onto her head, tucked her braids into the waistband, and then slipped on the mask to hold the makeshift wig in place. The red yarn strands dangled past her shoulders.

"You look great," Ann said.

"Let's go!" Katie cried impatiently.

Julie wearily trudged after her friends into the chilly evening air. All night she hung back from their chatter, too tired to form words. She parroted, "Trick or treat," at each house; she absently opened her brown paper sack for the treats. But she felt almost dizzy with the need for sleep. She couldn't wait to slide into soft pajamas, to lie beneath her fuzzy blankets, to set her aching head onto her cool pillows, and to slip into...

"Trick or treat!" a chorus of voices shouted in front of her.

"Trick or treat," Julie echoed hollowly, holding out her bag.

Soon, but not soon enough for Julie, the girls were walking up Bass Street with full sacks for a night of fun at Julie's house.

Mr. Drake, in a monkey costume, his mask hanging around his neck, was replacing a candle

stump in one of the jack-o-lanterns he carved all by himself last night. Usually Mr. Drake and Julie carved them together in the kitchen after dinner, while they sipped cinnamon-y hot cider Mrs. Drake made for them. But this year, Julie was behind with homework and could not help him.

"Hey, girls!" Mr. Drake cried as the girls approached the steps. "What do ghosts eat for breakfast?"

"I give up!" Katie exclaimed.

"Ghost Toasties – and evaporated milk," Mr. Drake said, laughing at his joke.

Katie giggled as she filed past him. Julie couldn't see Ann's reaction but guessed she smiled.

"Jules?" Mr. Drake asked.

"Very funny, Dad," Julie said as she stepped over the threshold.

"No treats until I inspect them," Mr. Drake called after them as they trooped into the kitchen.

Mrs. Drake was setting a lid on a saucepan. The room smelled like warm chocolate.

"I figured you girls might like some hot cocoa to warm you up," Mrs. Drake said as she opened the cupboard.

"Me! Me!" Katie shouted, waving her hand in the air and jumping up and down.

"Grow up, Katie," Ann said sternly.

Julie yawned behind her hand.

While Mrs. Drake poured hot cocoa into three blue mugs, the girls carefully laid their homemade

treats on the kitchen table. The act was more formality than concern for danger and more a reason for Mr. Drake to indulge on sweets. Dr. Rothgard had told Mr. Drake to watch what he ate. But Mr. Drake always "forgot," so Mrs. Drake always reminded him. So Mr. Drake carefully scanned the treats, even though everyone knew who made treats because they made them every year. Mrs. Cooper made the candy applies. Mrs. Dalton made the popcorn balls with Cara and Katie's help. Mrs. Drake had made the peanut butter cookies and the sugar cookies. Mrs. Brown had made the crisped rice and marshmallow squares. Mrs. Walker had made the brownies.

"Now let's see," Mr. Drake removed the wax paper wrapper from the first crisped rice bar. He took a bite and then held it up. "Safe! Next treat!"

Fifteen minutes later, the girls had finished their hot cocoa and Mr. Drake, having sampled all the treats and pronouncing them safe to eat, was settling in the living room to play Chinese checkers with Mrs. Drake. Julie slogged up the stairs after her friends. She could scarcely keep her eyes open.

That is what, ultimately, started the fight.

Katie had quickly flown out of her costume and into pajamas, eager to play her favorite board game with Ann and Julie, which Mr. Drake had removed from the shelf for her. But, somehow, Julie had fallen asleep across bed number one while taking her shoes off and woke with a heart-stopping

jolt when Katie screeched her name.

"You're mean!" Katie screamed. "Mean! Mean! Mean!"

Ann quickly shushed Katie but not soon enough. Mrs. Drake stormed onto the scene, demanding to know the trouble.

"No trouble," Ann said, while Julie rubbed her eyes and struggled to push past sleep waves to sit up. "Katie's just disappointed because Julie's too tired to play the game."

"Well," Mrs. Drake said with a worried glance at Julie. "Perhaps it's best she sleeps. Can't you play the game without her?"

Good idea, Julie thought, pulling the blanket up to her neck and drifting away.

"Yes." Ann's voice cut through the fog.

"It's more fun with Julie!" Katie wailed. "But she's too busy anymore. She only thinks about herself! She's mean! Mean and selfish!"

Julie bolted up and pointed her finger at Katie. "You're the mean one! Shut up! Let me sleep! Who cares about a stupid game?"

Katie picked the board and threw it; Julie ducked, and it landed soundlessly on the bed. Then Katie threw the paper money, which immediately fluttered to the ground. So Katie screamed until her face turned red and the cords on her face stuck out.

Ann sighed and turned away, disgusted.

But Katie's screaming went through Julie like an electric shock. She bounded off the bed, ready to

smack her, but Mrs. Drake held her back.

"Julie, go to bed," Mrs. Drake said quietly. "Katie, stop your tantrum right now. Or Mr. Drake will drive you home – right now."

Katie immediately stopped screaming. She put her face into her hands, sobbing and mumbling, "She's mean, mean, mean, mean."

"Katie, I mean it," Mrs. Drake said firmly in "that voice," the one that meant business. "Be quiet, or you're going home."

Katie's sobbing instantly turned to whimpering. Mrs. Drake paused a minute and then left, softly shutting the door behind her.

Ann stepped over the scattered game pieces to sit on bed number one with Julie and put her arm around Julie's shoulders. Katie lowered her hands, aghast that Ann was siding with Julie.

"You're BOTH mean," Katie whispered in her loudest voice.

"YOU'RE being mean," Ann said quietly. "You're nothing but a big baby. Julie is tired. We can play the game tomorrow."

"I want to play it tonight!" Katie hissed loudly. "I've looked forward to it all day! And now you're taking her side. You're mean too! I hate you, Ann Dalton!"

Julie swung her legs over the side of the bed. Alarmed, Katie cried, "Where are you going?"

"To get Dad," Julie snarled. "To take you home."

"Noooooooooooo!" Katie leaped over the game and onto the bed, grabbing Julie's arm. "I don't want to go home."

"Then shut up and go to bed." Ann spoke in a very low voice, so Mr. and Mrs. Drake wouldn't hear, but her blue eyes behind her black glasses flashed angrily. Her cheeks were flushed, too. "Go to bed right now, Katie Miller."

Katie let go of Julie and stomped to bed number two. "Fine! But you're still mean."

All anger drained from Julie as quickly as it flared up. She dropped to her side, folded a pillow over her head, and fell instantly asleep.

Julie wakened the next morning shortly before her friends. Through the early morning sunlight filtering through the curtains, Julie saw Ann sleeping on her back on bed number two and Katie curled up next to her. Julie scarcely recalled Katie's outburst; she'd been that tired. But as she watched her friends sleep, realization dawned on Julie. Katie didn't really think Julie was mean. Katie was simply missing the old times together.

So now on Sunday afternoons, the three girls snacked on popcorn, worked their way through any lingering assignments – and then some.

For the girls had figured out their teachers' habits and easily anticipated many of the next week's assignments. Working ahead helped Julie juggle her many responsibilities; working together gave Julie more time with her friends. If they worked

quickly, they sometimes had time for a card or board game or a bike ride in the washed-out November afternoon. That helped soothe Katie's hurt feelings and gave Julie an opportunity to hop off the eternal merry-go-around of school, library, piano, and homework.

However, nothing scared Julie more than the thought of oversleeping. Julie's new life didn't allow for a single misstep to the right or to the left. The shrill blast from Julie's alarm clock never failed to zap her with enough adrenaline to crawl sleepily out of bed.

So on this Thanksgiving Day, sitting at the Dalton's dinner table with her family and friends basking in the beauty of the lacy tablecloth, the chrysanthemum centerpiece, the soft glow from the yellow candles, and waiting for the mouthwatering feast to begin, Julie overflowed with gratitude.

For alarm clocks that worked.

For her job and all of Mrs. Clements' help.

For her parents – for finally understanding.

For piano lessons, yes, even those.

For her friends – especially Ann, who smiled at Julie as she passed the bowl of salted mixed nuts while Mr. Dalton carved the turkey and Mrs. Dalton and Mrs. Drake planned their Christmas crafts, and while Mr. Drake entertained Clay, Ann's five-year-old brother, with his latest cache of turkey riddle.

Julie had no idea what Ann said to Katie after Julie went to sleep on Halloween night. But Katie

had awakened subdued on November 1. Katie might not fully comprehend, like Ann did, Julie's dream. But Ann was used to working with her parents at Dalton's Dry Goods. It was harder for Katie, who was coddled at home, to accept Julie's new direction.

But Julie was mostly thankful with the knowledge that each day she inched closer to her goal of *Julie Drake, Psychologist.*

That night before she went to bed, Julie pulled out her dictionary from the bottom of her desk drawer. She opened to "psychologist," moved the newspaper clipping aside, and then picked up a pencil and circled the word "psychologist."

In the margin next to it, she wrote in ME in large letters. Then she closed the book, patted its cover with a smile, and went to bed.

CHAPTER 11: PEN AND PAPER

On Friday, Julie ate leftover turkey sandwiches for lunch at the Miller home while she, Ann, and Katie wrote out their Christmas gift list.

Mr. Drake had promised to drive them to Jenson tomorrow to see the Christmas decorations and purchase their presents. Ann and Katie were full of gift ideas and happily scribbled them onto the lined notebook paper in their spiral notebooks.

Mrs. Dalton's favorite cologne was Parterre de Fleurs, so Ann wanted to buy her a big bottle. Mr. Dalton, who liked trains, set up a miniature track around the tree every Christmas with Clay. Ann hoped to find "something" train-related; she just didn't know "what" yet. Clay loved monsters, but he hated reading. So Ann was on the hunt for a fun monster book with lots of pictures.

Katie's family handled gift-buying differently because her family was so large.

"We put our names in a bowl," Katie said. "We each pick one and buy that person a gift."

"Except your parents," Ann said as she wrote her ideas.

"Right. Cara and I and our brothers put our money together and buy one big gift for them."

"Do you know what you're getting yet?" Julie asked.

Katie nodded happily. "Yep. We're sending

them to the Wisten overnight."

The Wisten was an old historic hotel in Jenson that had an elegant restaurant on its first floor. The girls had never been inside, but Mr. Drake often drove past it when they went to the movies.

Ann took a bite of sandwich. "Whose name did you pick this time?"

"Eric. I wrote down some ideas." Katie held up her notebook so Ann and Julie could see.

Eric was seventeen and liked cars so much, he worked part time with Drake at the used car lot in Jenson. He was also very handsome, the most handsome of all Katie's brothers – and she had seven of those. Katie's gift ideas included a book about cars, a nice shirt, men's cologne, or a small transistor radio.

"If I can find one on sale," Katie added. "Eric likes music a lot. But he can't listen to it a lot. Mom and Dad only listen to the news." She leaned across the table. "What's on your list, Julie?"

Julie closed her notebook. "I'm still working on my list." She stuffed the final bite of her sandwich into her mouth and drained the last of her milk. "I have to go, or I'll be late for work." She picked up her apple. "I'll eat it along the way."

Katie stood, too. "We'll walk with you. Right, Ann?"

"Sure.

Usually Julie only worked on hour on Fridays. But Julie was going to Jenson tomorrow. So

because Julie had no school today, Mrs. Clement was letting Julie work five hours today. This way, Julie kept her bonus dollar, too.

The day was gray and cloudy, and Julie felt the cold through her jacket. The girls talked as they walked, and their breaths puffed white before them.

"When are we leaving?" Ann asked.

"Eight o'clock," Julie said. "Dad wants to get home early to beat the snow."

"Ooooh, I can't wait for the snow." Katie's cheeks were pink with cold and anticipation. "It's so pretty, and we can make ice cream again!"

"Snow is pretty," Julie agreed. "But Dad said the first snow of the year is extra slippery. He doesn't want to get stuck on the country roads."

"And your Mom is letting him still drive us?" Ann asked, blue eyes merry.

Julie scowled. She hated the way Mrs. Drake treated Mr. Drake like a little boy. And she hated the way he called her "mother." Ann knew it, too.

"She told him not to go," Julie admitted as they drew near Munsonville Library. "But he said he promised us. And then he promised her he'd be home before the first flake fell."

Katie's teeth were chattering. "I'm cold. Let's warm up before we go home."

"Good idea," Ann said.

Julie brooded about her Christmas shopping list all afternoon while she shelved books – or, rather, Julie's non-list. Julie had plenty of ideas for

gifts. Mr. Drake spent a lot of time outside, even in the winter. But he had trouble finding a hat that didn't creep up his ears. So Julie wanted to buy him a hat with earflaps. But he really liked board games; Julie knew he'd be thrilled with a new one. Mrs. Drake loved puzzles; the harder the puzzle, the more Mrs. Drake loved it. Mrs. Drake also needed new music books; the ones tucked inside the piano bench had faded to yellow, and the pages were falling out. Ann followed several mystery series, but it took Munsonville Library forever to get new books. So Ann usually saved her money to buy the books, which also took forever. Julie knew several Ann wanted; it was all a matter of choosing one. Katie longed for a set of electric curlers for practicing hairstyles. But the set cost fifteen dollars, which was a lot of money for one gift in a big family.

However, Julie had the money. She just didn't want to spend it.

So far, Julie had earned sixty dollars – but twelve dollars had gone to Mrs. Drake for piano lessons. That left Julie with forty-eight dollars toward her lessons at Jenson College, if its music professor accepted her. Julie had also saved another thirteen dollars this year from the "extras" Mr. Drake gave her from time to time and five dollars from helping Mrs. Drake with big projects around the house. That made sixty-six dollars altogether, a small fortune, in Julie's mind. It was about half of Mr. Drake's weekly paycheck, a fact she overheard

him tell Mrs. Drake the day he received a bonus for the most cars sold in the past month.

Julie's friends had even less money for gifts. Katie had ten dollars from her parents' Christmas Club at Village Hall. Ann had saved seventeen dollars, but she only worked when her parents needed extra help.

But if Julie bought Ann a new mystery book for two dollars, her mother a new puzzle for three dollars, her father a hat with flaps – or a board game – for four dollars – Julie would have just fifty-six dollars left. In addition, Mr. Drake had estimated the cost of gas to and from Jenson College would close one dollar each week. All these expenses made Julie very, very nervous. Yet, the thought of greeting her parents and friends on Christmas Day without any gifts made Julie's stomach very queasy under its turkey lunch. Julie loved the excitement of giving gifts. She loved finding the right gift. She loved wrapping gifts. She loved the delight on the faces of the people she loved when they opened her gift. Christmas would not be Christmas for Julie without any gifts to give.

But Julie couldn't bear to part with ten dollars – or more – of her very hard-earned money on gifts when she needed to save the money for piano lessons at Jenson College.

"Why must things cost so much?" she grumbled to herself and then stopped, shocked.

Why, Julie thought, I sound like my mother

after she buys our groceries or my father after he fills the car with gas.

Is that what it's like to be a grownup, Julie wondered as she placed a book on its proper place on the shelf. Mr. Drake worked hard at the used car lot in Jenson. He did the home repairs and kept the yard clean and tidy. Mrs. Drake worked hard at home, at Munsonville Inn, and for school and church events. Julie thought of all the times they told her "no" when she wanted this item or that item, items she couldn't recall now. Is that how they felt – loath to spend the money in case they ran out when they needed it?

By eight o'clock the next morning, Mr. Drake was kissing Mr. Drake's cheek good-bye and thanking her for a most delicious breakfast. It was nothing special, just oatmeal enriched by eggs that Mrs. Drake had stirred into the pot. Mrs. Drake said eggs made the oatmeal "stick to one's ribs." To Julie, eggs made cereal taste like custard. But it was filling, especially since Mrs. Drake topped it with tender baked apples and cinnamon sugar.

"Cold" Mr. Drake asked while he was waiting for the engine to warm up. He turned to her, grinning, and rubbing his hands together.

"A little," Julie said.

Julie scarcely noticed the cold. Her head ached from thinking about money versus gifts so much. She didn't want to go Christmas shopping in Jenson. She wanted to crawl under her blankets and

forget about – everything.

"This will warm you up. What do you call a dog on the beach in summer?"

Julie shrugged.

"A hot dog!" Mr. Drake nudged Julie's shoulder. "Get it?"

"Very funny, Dad."

Mr. Drake drove down Bass Street and up Blue Gill Road to pick up Katie. Then he drove down Blue Gill Road and up Pike Street to pick up Ann. Soon they were back down Pike Street and turning right onto Main Street, past the *Munsonville. Population: 386. Everyone Welcome Here* sign, and into the bare countryside on their way to Jenson. Mr. Drake had turned the radio to a station that played Christmas songs. But news reports of the upcoming snow interrupted the cheery carols and the sacred hymns during the entire trip.

Jenson was already packed with cars and pedestrians, even though store managers were just turning the door signs from CLOSED to OPEN. Mr. Drake drove around block after block looking for an empty parking spot. Finally, he stopped in front of a laundromat.

"Wait near the door while I park," Mr. Drake said. "I'll be right back."

They did as Mr. Drake instructed. The steamy room hummed with the sound of washers and dryers and smelled of warm clothes. Ann's glasses fogged up. They shivered against cold blasts whenever

someone opened the front door. An old man and several young mothers were folding laundry at the counter. One weary mom read a book to a toddler picking his nose. Two men sat in the back, chatted to each other. A college student, legs crossed at the knee, flipped through a fashion magazine, cracking her gum and swinging her foot.

"I'm glad we have our own washing machine and dryer," Ann said.

"Mommy still uses the wringer in the basement and hands the clothes on the line," Katie said. "But she doesn't mind."

Julie's house had a washer and dryer, too. She wondered how much they cost.

Soon, Mr. Drake popped into the laundromat to warm up. His face was red, and his nose was running with the cold. He reached into his pocket for a handkerchief and dabbed his nose dry.

"Ready?" he asked, holding the door open with a happy grin. Mr. Drake looked more excited than Katie.

"Yes!" Katie exclaimed.

They walked up and down the streets with the rest of the crowd and admired the colorful Christmas decorations. One store featured eight, very tiny reindeer pulling a sleigh filled with toys, while Santa waved a mechanical arm at shoppers. Another window offered a winter wonderland of snowflakes, snowmen, snowwomen, and mitten-clad dolls engaged in a mock snowball fight. A third

was full of games, trucks, and dolls, flanked by colorful packages tied with shiny bows and stacked in groups of threes, fours, and fives. A large window boasted a sleek electric train set running around the tracks of a North Pole scene, up hills, through tunnels, and around lakes. Another window has collector Victorian dolls.

On nearly every street corner, a Santa Claus rang a bell, and shoppers dropped coins into his bucket.

"Merry Christmas!" Santa called to each one, as he distributed candy canes.

Mr. Drake gave the girls dimes to they could get cold candy canes, which the girls slowly savored.

"It makes my mouth feel extra cold," Katie said, sucking the wind with a grin.

They did most of their shopping at Kylie's, a large department store that carried all the items on the girls' lists – including a transistor radio on sale for thirteen dollars and ninety-nine cents. Julie glumly wandered through the aisles, pretending to browse and not knowing what to do. At the end of one aisle was a box of assorted holiday greeting cards on sale for seventy-five cents. An idea jumped into Julie's head. She picked up a box and hurried to the counter.

Her friends suspiciously eyed her bag as they left the store

"That's all you're buying?" Ann asked.

"Yep."

"It's awfully small," Katie said doubtfully.

"Good things come in small packages," Mr. Drake quipped. "Speaking of small — what has lots of tiny needles but can't sew?"

"A Christmas tree," Ann said.

Mr. Drake blinked in surprise. "Whoa — you're a real smarty. Ready for lunch?"

"Yes!" Katie cried.

Mr. Drake led the way to Jenson Family Restaurant, where they ordered club sandwiches and hot chocolate. The speakers in the restaurant played Christmas music, barely audible over the chatter of the other patrons.

They were back on the road by early afternoon and passed the *Munsonville. Population: 386. Everyone Welcome Here* sign as the first flakes began to fall.

Mrs. Drake was so happy to see Mr. Drake she gave him a big hug at the back door.

"Mother," Mr. Drake said, beaming. "You should see…"

Julie slipped upstairs with her small bag; thankful she had the next few hours free. She'd have to tackle homework tonight, but for now…

To Katie's extreme disappointment, Julie begged off the Sunday homework club for "just this once" because Julie had "something to do" that afternoon.

Julie sped through her assignments as fast as she could, hoping her diligence might bring her good

luck.

But after Julie returned assignments and books to her plastic tote bag, Julie opened her notebook and began writing the letter, following the format from her English book.

7 Bass Street
Munsonville, MA, 98027

Jenson College of Liberal Arts
1 Palladium Drive
Jenson, MA, 98127

Dear Jenson College Music Department,

I am eleven years old and in the sixth grade at Munsonville School.

My mother is my piano teacher. She plays very well and is a good teacher.

Mrs. Clements at Munsonville Library said you accept some students for lessons.

I would like to take lessons with you. I have been working at the library to pay for lessons.

Please let me know how much lessons cost and if you will accept me.

I promise to practice a lot. I want to earn a scholarship.

Sincerely,

Julie Drake

On the Saturday before Christmas, Mr. Drake, Mr. Dalton, and Mr. Miller went to Simons Woods right after breakfast to find the right Christmas trees for their homes. Julie lazed on her bed with a ghost story with Muffy and Mittens curled up against her. It felt good to read again for fun now that school was closed until the new year, even though Julie had work in the afternoon. She stretched and turned a page. What luxury to do nothing!

After church the next day, Mr. Drake brought the tree into the living room and decorated it with Julie. They didn't hang any of their wooden ornaments near the bottom because the cats would knock them off. They also didn't hang any tinsel, just in a case a curious cat decided to try a bite.

Mrs. Drake baked Christmas cookies all afternoon and brought an assortment, still warm from the oven and sprinkled with melting red or green sugar, into the living room for Julie and Mr. Drake to much while they worked.

"It's a beautiful tree, Sam," Mrs. Drake said, pausing in her work to admire it. "I think it's the prettiest tree yet."

Mr. Drake lit up like a Christmas tree. "Mother, I'm glad you like it."

Julie frowned, hung another ornament, and said nothing.

They opened their gifts on Christmas morning before church services. Mrs. Drake had risen early to make cinnamon rolls for breakfast, which the family enjoyed with scrambled eggs and orange juice before settling near the softly lighted tree in the living room.

Mr. Drake had bought Mrs. Drake several new landscape puzzles and a beautiful necklace with a gold knot at the end. Mrs. Drake had bought Mr. Drake a new board game and a warm winter hat with flaps to keep his ears warm. Finally the only presents left were a small box with Julie's name on the tag and Julie's two greeting cards.

"Merry Christmas, Mom," Julie said, handing Mrs. Drake her card. "Merry Christmas, Dad."

Her parents glanced at each as they slipped their fingers beneath the envelope flaps to remove the cards.

As her parents opened the cards, their eyes grew very wide. Mr. Drake pulled out a sheet of paper and unfolded it, eyes filling with tears. Mrs. Drake cried, "Goodness!" and a shower of jagged paper pieces fell into her lap and onto the floor.

For Julie had designed a miniature board game on a piece of paper for Mr. Drake with each of the squares featuring one of his riddles. And Julie had written a note of appreciation to Mrs. Drake for her mother and then cut the note into puzzle pieces for Mrs. Drake to assemble.

"We'll need dice from a real game to play it,"

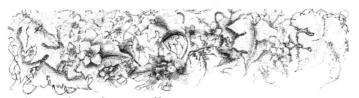

Julie said apologetically.

Mr. Drake smiled, but his lip quivered. "But we have to play this afternoon."

"Sure, Dad."

Mrs. Drake pointed to the small box. "You haven't opened your gift, Julie."

Wondering, Julie reached for the box, untied the ribbon, and removed the wrapping. She lifted the lid and gasped aloud. For inside the box was a little passbook to the First Bank of Jenson, and inside that passbook was a deposit for fifty dollars.

"Your father and I talked," Mrs. Drake said. "We don't understand your dream. But we're proud of your hard work and want to support it."

Mr. Drake put on a mock stern face. "But you better use it for college, Jules. Or else."

"Deal!" Julie cried.

It was the best Christmas ever.

She gave Ann and Katie their gifts in the narthex after church. Ann and Katie had a shared gift for Julie: an IOU for lunch at Sue's Diner during Christmas vacation, their treat.

"We want to reward you," Katie said, her eyes sparkling. "You've worked so hard."

Now it was Ann and Katie's turn to be surprised. Ann's card had a one-page mystery story Julie had written just for her, which Ann quickly skimmed.

"This is very good," Ann said, refolding her story and slipping it back into her card. "I didn't

know you wrote stories."

"I didn't either until I tried."

Katie also had an IOU: one full day that Julie, Katie, and Ann would spend together during Christmas break, doing whatever Katie wanted to do and eating whatever food Katie wanted to eat.

With a squeal, Katie pounced on Julie and hugged her hard. "You're the bestest friend ever!"

The winter and early spring of 1970 looked a lot like the fall of 1969. Julie still rode the merry-go-round of school, work, piano lessons, and homework. But the merry-go-around shone less brightly. Julie had never heard from Jenson College.

"Don't be discouraged," Mrs. Clements said when Julie once again answered "not yet" to Mrs. Clements. "These things take time."

Finally the day arrived for the final test of Julie's sixth grade year, her math test. Math was still hard for Julie and still not her favorite subject. Ann and Katie completed the test before Julie did and were quietly leafing through the pages of their library books. Julie knew she'd never compute as fast as Ann and Katie. But Julie was learning to be a more efficient Julie, and this made her happy

A jumble of thoughts jumped around Julie's head as she signed her name and rose to walk the test to Mrs. Fitzgerald's desk. She felt a pang of sadness at her final sixth grade math test and realized that, somewhere along the way, she'd stopped dreading math. Sometimes, Julie even

enjoyed the challenge of solving the problems.

Solving the problems.

Why, Julie thought with sudden realization, math was just another form of problem-solving – and so was improving her piano playing, budgeting her money, and balancing her time between all the facets of her life.

Julie thought back to "Dream Ghouls" and how glamorous it had seemed to be a psychologist and solve people's problems.

Julie thought back to all the problems her dream created for her.

And then Julie thought about all her experiences along the way to solving those problems. No matter her final grades, Julie had really learned a lot in the sixth grade.

With a deep breath, Julie handed her test to Mrs. Fitzgerald.

CHAPTER 12: LAUREL WREATH

Mrs. Drake woke up on Sunday morning with bad cold and asked Julie to "fill in" for her at Munsonville Congregational Church that morning.

Julie almost choked on her cornflakes.

"But – Mom!" Julie's heart pounded hard. "I can't play in church in front of everyone. I'm not even that good yet."

Mrs. Drake grabbed her handkerchief and sneezed hard.

"But services won't be the same without music," Mrs. Drake insisted. You play several hymns very well."

Julie said nothing.

"If it's too hard for you, then just forget it."

That did it.

Julie looked straight at her mother. "It's not too hard. You get some rest. I'll play for services."

Munsonville Congregational Church was a plain church: whitewashed walls, board floors worn smooth with the years, and straight block pews. The alter area, a simple raised platform, contained only a podium and unadorned wood cross. To the right near the front stood an old piano, the piano Julie would play that morning.

She sat on that hard wooden bench, shaking down to her shoes. Even her fingers trembled. Just what Julie needed. The whole church would hear her

mistakes.

An overweight Reverend Brown stood panting at the front end of the church and clutching his service book to his chest. He had the same tousled brown hair as his son Joey Brown, Julie's classmate.

Reverend Brown nodded to Julie.

She took a huge breath to calm her racing heart, positioned her hands over the keys, and struck the first notes of *Amazing Grace*. Halfway through, a Julie noticed how automatically she played it, as if her fingers didn't need her brain at all.

That's why piano players practice so much, Julie thought, amazed at yet another new insight.

Now in-between the hymns, while Reverend Brown preached, Julie sat on that bench shaking like a stalk in the wind. But all anxiety fled the moment Julie began to play. Now if Julie allowed herself to think about the playing, she did strike wrong notes. So she worked on simply letting her fingers do the work and not thinking too much. Luckily, Julie faced the altar area. She didn't have to see the entire village sitting behind her, watching her play.

During announcements, Reverend Brown said Mrs. Drake had a cold and asked for prayers.

"Fortunately, we had a very talented pianist this morning. Please stop and thank Miss Julie Drake before you leave."

Julie gulped.

But she obediently rose.

For fifteen minutes, Julie stood at the piano and accepted the everyone's praise, including that of her teachers and the parents of her classmates.

"You're really good, "Ann said, giving Julie a hug and then stepping aside so Katie could, too.

"Weren't you scared?" Katie breathed, eyes wide. "I'd be so scared."

"I was," Julie admitted. "A little."

Mr. Drake stepped up next.

"You really blew them over, Jules," Mr. Drake said. "Hey, who was the most popular actor in the Bible?"

"Not now, Dad," Julie whispered.

"Samson. Because he brought the house down." Dr. Drake poked Julie's shoulder. "Get it?"

For lunch that afternoon, Julie made peanut butter and banana sandwiches for her and Mrs. Drake and heated up some chicken soup for her mother. Julie brought the soup upstairs on a little tray while Mr. Drake set up the cribbage game.

"Are you feeling better, Mom?"

"A little," Mrs. Drake said. "My throat doesn't hurt as much, and my cough is better."

"Good. Get some rest, Mom."

Mrs. Drake clapped her hand to her forehead. "Julie! I forgot! You have a package."

Julie's heart started to pound. "A package?"

"Yes. A thick manilla envelope. I set the mail on my desk yesterday and forgot all about it."

Julie walked to Mrs. Drake's desk and then let out a surprised and happy whoop.

"Mom!" Julie waved the envelope in the air. "It's from Jenson College!"

"Open it! Wait – call your father!"

So Julie called for Mr. Drake to come upstairs so they could read the news together. Julie's heart sank as she read the letter aloud. Lessons were held Thursdays after school and cost ten dollars. Ten dollars! For one lesson! Julie couldn't afford that! What a blow after she'd work so hard!

"Hold on a minute Julie Girl," Mr. Drake said. "The program also has a scholarship." He held up several sheets of paper. "You can apply for a reduced rate of five dollars a week."

Julie quickly did the math in her head. If she lost one day of work plus the bonus dollar, she'd earn eight dollars a week. If she received the scholarship, she'd still have two dollars left over each week after lessons and gas. It was do-able, if Jenson College granted her a scholarship,

"You also need two recommendations, one from her music teacher and one who could attest to her character," Mr. Drake continued.

Julie looked hopefully at Mrs. Drake. "Mom?"

"Of course, I'll recommend you." Then Mrs. Drake started coughing and reached for a handkerchief.

"You will also need to audition in front of the music department, too." Mr. Drake set the letter

down. "Aren't you glad you got warmed up today?"

"Am I ever!" Then Julie thought of something. "Thursday after school? How will I get back and forth?"

"Steve Barnes drives into Jenson at least once a week for supplies," Mr. Drake said. "I'll ride with him and leave your mother the car. She can drive you."

"And then we can pick you up after the lesson!" Julie gave him a big hug.

Mrs. Drake's eyes drooped. "I think I'll take a nap. Julie, please remove the tray."

Monday was the last day of school, and it was a half day, just long enough to hand out report cards and enjoy cupcakes in the lunchroom to celebrate. Of course, some students wept instead of smiled due to their poor grades. Julie had peeked at her report card and then immediately shoved it back inside her envelope. She couldn't think about it now. She'd start crying if she did.

Unbeknownst to Julie, Ann and Katie had collected gum wrappers from everyone they knew and wove them into a long chain on those long weekday nights when Julie studied alone. They hung that chain around Julie's neck like a laurel wreath.

"For all your hard work," Katie said with a big smack on Julie's cheek.

Julie fingered a gum wrapper. For all her hard work, Katie had said. Ann and Katie were proud of Julie's hard work. Results mattered but

hard work mattered, too, didn't it?

She walked slowly home from school, savoring the minty/fruity smells of the papers draping her neck. She opened the back door where Mr. and Mrs. Drake sat at the kitchen table drinking tea. Mrs. Drake was feeling better, but Mr. Drake now had her cold and stayed home because Mrs. Drake insisted.

"Well?" Mrs. Drake asked.

Julie waved her report card. "I got my first A! In math!"

And the warmth that flowed through Julie at saying those words was warmer and brighter than the Munsonville sun on that sunny June day.

Denise M. Baran-Unland is the author of the phantasmic BryonySeries, which includes the "drop of blood" vampire trilogy for young and new adults, a Gothic prequel for adults, the Limbo trilogy, a standalone werewolf novel, the Adventures of Cornell Dyer chapter book series for grade and middle school students, the Girls of the BryonySeries series for tween girls, and the Bertrand the Mouse series for young children.

She has six adult children, three adult stepchildren, seventeen total grandchildren, six godchildren, and four cats.

She is the co-founder of WriteOn Joliet and has published several anthologies for the group. She previously taught features writing for a homeschool coop, with the students' work published in the co-op magazine and The Herald-News in Joliet.

Denise blogs daily and is currently the features editor at The Herald-News. To read her feature stories, visit theherald-news.com.

For more information about Denise's writings and to follow her on social media, visit bryonyseries.com and dmbaranunland.co

120

Jennifer Wainwright is a self-taught artist whose talented bloomed in junior high art class when she learned proper shading and her teacher challenged her to "think outside the box."

She works in various mediums, including photography, paint, charcoals and pottery, but prefers ink, pastels and clay. Jennifer especially loves creating art for others, to bring their vision to life.

Jennifer created the "Welcome to Munsonville" illustration of "Main Street" that greets visitors to the BryonySeries website. She also created the frontispiece for the standalone BryonySeries novel "Lycanthropic Summer" and the cover art for the "Girls of the BryonySeries" series for tween girls.

Message her at jenniboom94@gmail.com or through me at bryonyseries@gmail.com.